Education Curriculum Center
The Ohio State University at Newark
Hopewell 84
1179 University Drive
Newark, Ohio 43055

HOW MANY MILES
TO SUNDOWN

For Olivia E. King and
Mary Louise Archambault

PATRICIA BEATTY

HOW MANY MILES TO SUNDOWN

Frontispiece by Robert Quackenbush

William Morrow and Company   New York   1974

Printed in the United States of America.
6   7   8   9   10

Library of Congress Cataloging in Publication Data

Beatty, Patricia.
    How many miles to sundown.

    SUMMARY: In 1881 a tomboy, her younger brother, and
her pet longhorn accompany a fifteen-year-old boy searching
for his father through Texas and the New Mexico and Arizona
territories.
    [1. The   west—Fiction]   I.   Title.
PZ7.B380544Ho   [Fic]   73-14583
ISBN 0-688-20102-4
ISBN 0-688-30102-9 (lib. bdg.)

CONTENTS

1 THE HORSEBACKER

Because she was already way up in the big tree that shaded the porch, Beulah Land Quiney was first to see the rider in the distance. "There's a horsebacker comin'," she shouted down to Leo and Elnora. Then she reached out for the horseshoe Leo had tossed over the tree branch, carefully lifted it off, and sighted down through the leaves. She let the horseshoe fall just as close to her brother's russet head as she could without hitting him. What Beulah Land did, she tried to do well.

"You're tryin' to kill me, Beeler. Nothin's trickier than a redheaded female woman like you," Leo yelled at her, shaking his fist but moving out of the line of fire in case she let something else fall out of the pecan tree.

Beulah Land laughed as she tightened the belt on her pants. She reached out with a bare foot for the crotch of the tree, wedged her foot into it, and pulled herself out onto a limb. There she swung, just out of Leo's reach, while he took swipes at her feet with his hat, yelling all the time at her. J.E.B. Stuart, the black-and-white dog, pranced around Leo, barking his fool head off.

Elnora cried over the uproar, "Be careful, Beeler. You're gonna fall. Leo'll take the pitchfork to ya." The little girl flung her apron up over her face in fright.

"No, Leo won't." Beulah Land swung farther out and let go. She dropped, landing in a little pile of hay under the branch. There she stood, hitching up her pants, tucking in her shirt next, all the time staring her brother down. "Leo, I'm two years older'n you and a lot smarter. I can still lick the stuffin' outa you anyday. So you better wilt and beg for mercy."

Backing away, Leo shouted, "Holy Snakes, Beeler. You're on the prod today, ain't ya?"

"No, I ain't. You threw that horseshoe up in the tree 'cause Elnora was winnin' your game. I went up and got it down, so she can keep right on beatin' you fair and square the way she was doin'. Or mebbe you'd like me to whip you at horseshoes again?"

Leo was sullen. "I wish old Parker was here to whip you."

"Well, our big old brother Parker ain't here. He's laid up in the doctor's house in town, and that's six miles ridin' from this here ranch. He's gonna be there in Cottonwood for a long time. His bein' gone makes me the oldest Quiney to home. And right now with him all busted up I could lick him, too, even if he's fifteen and two years older'n me. Don't you forget I can lick any Quiney here in Santa Rosa County right now—except for our biggest brother of 'em all. And he ain't here neither!"

"Sure, Beeler's the biggest Quiney here right now for a fact," added carrot-topped Elnora, who was eight. She pulled at her sister's shirt sleeve. "Beeler, didn't you say there was a horsebacker comin' here?"

Beeler gave her favorite sister a grin. "Yep, he's comin' from the south. He ain't ridin' fast. It don't appear to be anybody we know."

"Mebbe it's yer fairy prince on a white horse comin' to get ya," Leo mocked.

"Nope, it's just a plain brown horse with a plain ordinary man on it. The sorta man you're gonna turn into if ya live that long, Leo."

"Ya know, Beeler," remarked the boy, "when you get mad, your face gets so red your freckles don't show no more. You oughta be mad all the time. Then you wouldn't look so ugly."

Beeler pointed at him but spoke to Elnora. "Look at him. He's grinnin' like a jackass eating cactus. Come on, Sis, we'll tell Nerissa somebody's on his way here. Leo, you go get the barn Winchester, you hear me?"

While Leo stalked angrily to the barn, followed by J.E.B. Stuart, the two girls went toward the low wooden ranchhouse. Elnora put her arm around her sister's waist and said, "He's only funnin' you, Beeler. You ain't truly ugly. You ain't so ugly and skinny as a new-sheared sheep the way he says, and it ain't true one bit if you didn't have long hair nobody'd take you for a girl. I think you're right pretty. You're what the preacher's wife in Cottonwood calls a strawberry blonde." Elnora reached up and tugged at one of her sister's yellow-red braids tied at the end with rawhide thongs. There just wasn't any getting Beeler to use hair ribbons.

"Elnora, I ain't much for pretty, but I'm surely active. I don't pay no real heed to Leo. I got the best-trained horse in Santa Rosa County, haven't I? I'd rather have Jinglebob than yellow curls and blue eyes that melt a man down."

Beeler opened the front door of the house and preceded her sister inside. She spoke to the tiny, frowning, dark-eyed woman who'd come at once to stand in the kitchen doorway as if she was guarding the larder. "Nerissa," said Beeler, "there's a rider comin' here. I seen him from the top of a pecan tree. I don't know him by sight. Mebbe he ain't friendly. We better get ready for him."

Nerissa, who'd married the oldest Quiney of them

all, sighed and said, "Oh, Beulah Land, I don't much
fancy anyone coming here with Earl gone away to the
mule market in Saint Louis. I wish we raised something besides mules. Saint Louis is such a long way
from here. We're all alone today—the six of us. I wish
to heaven your mother and father hadn't died. Even
if your older brothers and sisters *are* out on their own,
you youngest ones are a terrible responsibility to me."
She sighed again, wiped her hands on her apron, and
stepped to the wall, taking the house Winchester down
from its pegs.

"Leo's got the one from the barn," volunteered
Elnora.

The woman and both girls went out onto the long
porch. First of all they looked to see where Leo was.
He was standing guard beside the barn, out of sight,
with the other Winchester. Satisfied that he was ready
to greet a possibly hostile visitor who might know Earl
Quiney wasn't home, they looked south toward the
horsebacker.

"Where'd Lucy and Polly get to?" Beeler asked all
at once.

Her sister-in-law told her, "I sent them to the
orchard to pick early cherries for a pie tonight. Now
you be quiet, girls. Whoever is riding here is almost
at the gate. You let me do the talking to him."

"Draw a good bead on him," warned Beeler.

Strangers could mean lots of trouble in this part of Texas. Everybody in Santa Rosa County knew that and greeted strangers with suspicion just to be always on the safe side.

The woman held the rifle steady on the rider as he stopped just outside the white painted gate. He called out, "Howdy, Miz Quiney."

"Who'd you be, Mister?" cried Nerissa.

"Jonathan Graber. Parker knows me."

"Parker isn't here. Where did you know Parker?"

"Up north—a couple years ago." The horsebacker took off his hat to show yellow hair. He wasn't old at all—only a colt, too—not much older than Beulah Land herself.

Beeler watched her sister-in-law lower the rifle. "I guess it *must* be the Graber boy," Nerissa muttered. She called out to Leo, "It's all right. Don't shoot him. I think he's a friend of Parker's." Next she called to the rider, "Come on in."

Beeler watched, racking her memory. Then all at once it came to her. Parker had talked sometimes about a fat scrub with yellow hair by the name of Graber that he'd gone up north with two years before. This one was fat enough, and he had yellow hair too. "Take your finger outa your mouth," she told Elnora. "We got comp'ny."

Jonathan Graber dismounted, opened the gate, and

came through leading his horse. Grinning, he walked
to the porch, whipped off his hat again, and bowed to
Nerissa and the girls. "Your servant, ladies. I won't
trouble you folks. It's Parker I'm looking for. Where
can I find him?"

"Not here." Nerissa shook her head. "He's in Cottonwood." She gestured toward Beeler and Elnora.
"I've heard about you from Parker, but I don't think
you've ever met any other Quineys, have you? This is
Beulah Land and Elnora, and, oh, here's Leo now."

Beeler examined Graber carefully while he and
Leo howdied and shook. He was more broad than tall
and wore a leather jacket and pants and a big Mexican-
style hat. He face was pale under it, and his eyes were
a bright blue.

A wild barking took Beeler's attention from the
stranger as J.E.B. Stuart came dashing up to the porch.
He flung himself upon Graber, pawing his leg and
letting out howls of joy. "Hey, there's old J.E.B. I
know you, too, boy. Do you remember me, huh?"
asked Graber. He dropped to one knee to let the dog
run his tongue over his face. Beeler had to admit that
he understood about dogs. And J.E.B.'s recognizing
him proved just fine to her he was somebody who knew
Parker all right. J.E.B. was more Parker's dog than
anybody else's.

When Graber straightened up, he asked Nerissa,

"Where can I find Parker in Cottonwood, ma'am?"

"In the doctor's house—flat on his back."

Elnora added, "Every bone in his body's busted."

Seeing the look of shock on the Graber boy's face, Beeler explained, "He busted a arm and a leg tryin' to be a horsebreaker. It ain't as if he's dyin'. He's jest layin' there."

Graber made a sour face. "He said once he wanted to break horses. That's too bad he got hurt. I guess I'll have to go on alone then."

Leo perked up. "Go where?" he asked, as he leaned against a porch post with the Winchester under his arm.

"To Sundown."

Nerissa asked, "Where is that? I never heard of it."

Graber shook his head. "I don't know, but I think it's where my father is or where he's headed. He went down to the silver mines in Old Mexico three years ago. I stayed up north in Comanche country for two years without any word from him. I thought he must be dead until I got a letter from him last winter, asking me to come down to the town of Santa Inez in the state of Durango. But when I got there, he wasn't around anymore. They said he'd gone away north— they didn't know where for sure—perhaps to a place called Puesta del Sol. That name translates both ways— to Sundown or Sunset. All I know is that wherever it is, it's north of the border. A Mexican said *norte*, and there isn't any problem knowing what that means."

"And you wanted Parker to hunt for your pa with you?" asked Beeler.

"Well, I hoped he might." Graber had a mighty mournful look on his face, Beeler thought, but then he was entitled to have it. He'd made a long ride for nothing.

"I'll ride with ya," Leo offered. "Mebbe we can be gone all summer and fall and winter, so I won't have to go to Cottonwood to that there school. Schoolin's for womenfolks—not men."

"Leo Augustus Quiney!" Nerissa spun around, her hand ready to slap. She let it fall, though, and shook her head. "I'm sorry, Jonathan, Leo can't go. He's only eleven years old."

Beeler added, "He's a runt, too. I'm the biggest one to home right now."

"Full of vinegar, too," growled Leo. "She don't even mind the Cottonwood schoolmarm much."

Elnora piped, "Beeler don't mind nobody—even Nerissa—unless she's got a mind to."

Nerissa let out her breath, then said, "Well, Jonathan, at least you can take supper with us and stay overnight. I'm sorry we can't help you more, but we can do that much." She gave the three listening Quineys a warning glance. "You behave now, you hear me?" She spoke to Graber again. "I'd like to have you stay. It will be pleasant to hear good grammar and see good table manners for a change. Parker always did say you knew fingers from forks."

As Leo led away Graber's horse, Beeler asked, "What do you folks do up in Comanche country?"

He smiled. "Homestead and raise wheat."

"Sodbusters!" snorted the girl.

"That is enough of that," came from Nerissa. Beeler watched her sister-in-law go up to the door and stand there so Graber could open it for her. Shocked, Beeler pinched Elnora. "You keep your eyes peeled and watch how he stabs around with his fork while he's eatin'."

"Mebbe he'll stick the fork into Nerissa's hand tryin' to spear a biscuit, the way Leo does," Elnora said hopefully.

The girls waited together until Leo returned after putting Graber's horse in the corral. Beeler saw his long face and said, "This here Graber's a elegant gent, Leo. Here's a chance to watch him and better yerself. I know what you're thinkin'. You're feelin' ornery because you ain't goin' away with him tomorrow. But you're too much of a sprout yet. I'm the one who could go with him if I wasn't a girl. I'm the right age. You ain't."

Leo shot her a look of fury. "It ain't from lack of wishful thinkin' that you ain't a boy."

Beeler knew that he didn't like the way she was dressed. Nobody did. Well, that was just too bad. She was mighty comfortable wearing Parker's old shirt and pants, even if they were a mite big. Parker didn't need anything but a nightshirt where he was—just lolling in bed at the doctor's house. By the time the doc sent him back home, Beeler guessed she would have worn the elbows out of his shirt and the seat out of his britches. School had been out a couple of weeks now, and she hadn't had a skirt tripping her up or flopping around her ankles once. She could jump on Jinglebob anytime she had a mind to—something a female couldn't do in skirts unless she rode sidesaddle the way Nerissa did. Beeler wanted to spit thinking of sidesaddles but didn't. She didn't want Elnora to catch the habit.

Nate Graber and Nerissa did almost all of the talking at supper. First about Parker's being bucked off a horse and then about books they'd both read. Leo, who was angry, kept his eyes fixed on his plate. But Beeler and her younger sisters kept theirs glued to every fancy move Graber made with his knife, fork, and spoon.

Not that it was easy for Graber and Nerissa to talk over the outside noises. J.E.B. Stuart had been thrown out of the house that night because Nerissa was putting on elegant airs for company. J.E.B. yapped and dug at the kitchen door with his claws all during supper, wanting inside like usual. But when they got to the cherry pie, there came a different sound—a thudding and thumping on the front porch.

"He wants in again, Beeler," said Elnora.

Beeler saw Nate rise up out of his chair, still hanging politely onto his napkin. "What's that?"

Elnora answered him, yelling over J.E.B. Stuart's loudest howl yet and the thumping, "It's only Beeler's critter come up on the porch."

"Oh Lord, is he back?" Nerissa moaned.

"He never goes far away," said Beeler.

"Not far enough anyhow," added Leo in the first words he'd said all evening.

"But what is it?" asked Graber, as the thumping switched to a terrible stomping sound.

"It's a animal of the cow tribe," Beeler explained.

Nerissa took a swallow of coffee. "Pay it no heed, Jonathan. It can't get in. I thought I was marrying only Earl Quiney two years ago. He never bothered to tell me he had so many brothers and sisters still living at home without parents. They were a rude surprise to a bride from Fort Worth, let me tell you. I became a stepmother before I really felt like a bride." She sighed deeply. "I would have liked to feel like a bride. Earl deceived me." Recovering herself, Nerissa said more briskly, "Now don't you know anything really definite about the place your father is supposed to have gone to?''

Nate shook his head. "Only what I told you—that it's north over the border. North of Santa Inez. I know that for a fact because I used to live in Old Mexico and I speak some Spanish. My father was traveling north with four men, all of them Americans. Gringos, the Mexicans told me. And the four of them were pretty strange looking too. I've been asking about five men riding together wherever I've gone, but nobody seems to remember seeing them. A lot of folks south of here, though, have talked to me about the new towns springing up in northwest Texas. They say a lot of men are headed that way nowadays. So I'm going to look for my father up there."

Nerissa looked somber. "Yes, we've heard about those towns too. But they're quite a distance from here. What will you do if you don't find your father there?"

"Go back to the homesteaders who took me in a while back. They're fine people, ma'am."

"Humph," came from Beeler. "Sodbusters! Like I said before, you sure don't look like no sodbuster in that fancy Mexican rig you got on."

Sodbusters wore shoes. Cowboys wore high-heeled boots. Sodbusters walked in the dirt behind a horse and plow, which was a pretty disgraceful thing to do.

Cowboys never walked at all if they could help it. A man on horseback was superior to a man on foot, and most Texas people knew it.

Nate smiled. "I got these clothes down in Mexico. What I had on wore out by the time I got down there. These work out all right for me. I'm traveling light. Leather wears fine—better than cloth. All I need is my horse and some food."

Beeler watched Leo raise his bushy russet head from memorizing the yellow roses on his dinner plate. He said loudly, "Travelin' light! That's the only way for a man to get where he's goin' fast. A bag of grub, a fryin' pan and coffee pot, and good-enough horse. That's all a body could want in the summertime in Texas!"

Beeler left the supper dishes to Elnora and the other weaner gals. Elnora was plenty big enough to work the kitchen pump while the others washed and scoured. Nerissa didn't have to ride herd on them because she had them buffaloed. She could entertain company in the parlor. Beeler went to the horse corral with a carrot stolen from the root celler. She called out softly the way she always did, and Jinglebob came trotting right up to the bars to nose her hand for the carrot. He was plenty smart and plenty fast, even if he wasn't the handsomest horse there ever was. Beeler stroked the white blaze on the bay's forehead for a time, murmuring to him. She vowed Jinglebob could almost answer her.

And then she saw the other two horses in the corral. They were standing side by side at the far end in the darkness as if they were whispering to one another. One was Graber's brown horse. The other was Two Cents, Leo's big-headed buckskin with a Roman nose and no sense at all. He was usually leaning up against the corral, too lazy to stand by himself. Oh, they were a pair. Nate had talked about his horse at supper. He'd called the brown gelding Estupido in Mexico and Stupid in Texas. No wonder he got along so well with Two Cents. They were both coyotes—though coyotes were smarter.

Beeler told Jinglebob, "Don't you have nothin' to do with them two!"

J.E.B. Stuart joined her as she passed the barn and henhouse. "Did you get run off by my critter again?" she asked the dog. "You know how he is. You better keep outa his way. It's in his nature to hate dogs. And he's a good mite bigger'n you are now, J.E.B." Patting the dog's fur, Beeler stood beside the pecan tree listening to the music coming from the house. Nerissa was playing the cottage organ that had come on a wagon from Fort Worth last Christmas. It had been a present from her husband. He surely doted on that woman.

While she listened to "Beautiful Dreamer," Beeler saw the kitchen door open at the side of the house. Leo came out. He walked hunched over, with his hands in his pockets, to the bunkhouse where he and the other Quiney boys slept. J.E.B. Stuart streaked from Beeler's side to jump up at Leo's leg. J.E.B. had always favored the company of menfolks. Beeler kept silent to hear Leo's words to the dog. "By Gatlins, you old flea trap, we ain't knocked all the way back on our hocks yet, are we?" She watched them head for the corral.

For a moment she debated walking after Leo but decided not to. It would be useless. And speaking of something being useless, where was that critter now? She put two fingers into her mouth to whistle. But the music going on in the house stopped her. It was too pretty to spoil, and besides Nerissa hated that whistle. It was loud enough to wake the dead.

"Travis," Beeler called out softly, "Travis."

She waited, but nothing showed up out of the darkness. She figured what had happened. "Poor animal," she muttered to herself. "I bet he heard what Nerissa said about him bein' a tribulation to her. I bet he's out in the dark orchard right now feelin' as mournful as the way Nerissa makes me feel sometimes."

The first thing Beeler always did the minute she

got out of bed was look out her window at the corral, which was on her side of the house. That was to see how Jinglebob was. This morning she was a little bit anxious about him. That brown horse of Graber's, the strange one in the corral, might have pestered Jinglebob so he didn't get his rest. As soon as she'd done some of the barn chores for Nerissa, Beeler planned to ride Jinglebob out to look over the young mules that hadn't gone to market. They were ranging somewhere south of the house, according to Leo, who'd spotted them a couple of days ago. Beeler pulled back the white muslin curtain Nerissa had put up to block the view. There wasn't a horse in sight in the corral— except for old Two Cents leaning against the bars again, looking weary. That didn't mean anything, though. Jinglebob could be over at the water trough. As for Graber's horse, Graber was supposed to have left at dawn. Nerissa had even put up saddlebag food for him.

The girl hauled on shirt and pants and a pair of boots Leo had outgrown the year before. Her hair still in braids arranged yesterday, she slapped a hat of Parker's on her head. It was an old brown one she'd dolled up with a band of braided leather and some green wooden beads to make it fancier. She went downstairs as quietly as she could so as not to wake Nerissa up. Nerissa slept until 7 a.m. whenever she got the chance—which is what came of being born and bred in Fort Worth. City folks had city ways. Beeler didn't worry about disturbing her sisters. She knew that Elnora was already up and about, because she and Beeler shared a bed. All there'd been to remind her of Elnora's presence that morning had been a dent in the other pillow.

Beeler went out the kitchen door. She shooed the chickens away, vowing to make Elnora feed them later, and started for the corral to say good morning to Jinglebob. On the way she met Elnora.

Her finger in her mouth, Elnora was looking thoughtful. She took her finger out and asked Beeler, "Guess what's happened?"

"What?"

"That fat Graber scrub, he's gone." Elnora twirled around on her toes to walk with her sister.

"I figured he'd light out early," Beeler told her.

"That ain't all that's happened, though."

"What else?"

"Leo, he's gone with Graber. I been up for a long, long time. I heard Graber's horse makin' noises before sunup, kicking the corral. Leo told me to tell you all *adiós,* and he'd take good care of Jinglebob."

"*My horse?*" All at once Beeler felt sick all over. She looked through the rails of the corral. There wasn't any horse by the water trough. There wasn't any horse at all but Two Cents. "Elnora, you mean that son of a goat Leo took my horse?"

"Uh-huh. I seen him ridin' Jinglebob away."

"Why didn't you come get me? Why didn't he take his own horse?"

"He asked me not to say he was goin'. He made me promise him. He said mebbe he'd have a long way to go. He lit out after Graber, but they didn't ride off together. Graber, he went first."

Beeler grabbed her sister's arm. "He ain't gettin' away with it, takin' my horse. That's horse stealin'. I'm goin' after him."

"After Leo, Beeler?"

"No, not after that no-account brother. I'm goin' after Jinglebob. And you're gonna help me."

Elnora had a wispy tangle of brown-red hair in her mouth. She chewed it for a time, then said, "All right. Leo did a bad thing. I will if you want me to, Beeler."

"I surely do. Us womenfolks have got to stick together at times. You get me some supplies, and we'll leave a letter for Nerissa."

Elnora let out a wail. "Beeler, I can't write that good yet so she could read it."

"I didn't have it in mind for you to have to write it, Elnora. That's for me to do. It'll show up Leo plenty, my bein' polite enough to leave a letter. You talk to Nerissa after I've left and tell her what she wants to know. Now you get me a bag of grub, bacon and beans and coffee. And a skillet and two pans. I can boil my coffee."

Beeler was thinking rapidly. She'd get the money she'd made from selling eggs in Cottonwood. It was under the bed in a leather poke. She'd take Parker's sheepskin jacket and the six-shooter that was under the pink satin cushion in the parlor. She asked Elnora, "I bet Leo stole the barn Winchester, didn't he?"

"He took it. I saw it stuck onto his saddle."

"Get a-goin', Elnora."

Starting to move, the little girl asked, "Are you goin' to be takin' the wagon, Beeler?"

"Nope. I'll be travelin' light, too." Beeler ran for the house with Elnora trotting behind her. That miserable varmint of a Leo Quiney! Chasin' after Graber, lookin' for fun and stealin' a horse that wasn't his!

Elnora cried as she caught up with her, "Leo took J.E.B. Stuart, too!"

Beeler hissed, "That's just like Leo. Rob the whole roost! J.E.B.'s the best dog in Santa Rosa County. I could cuss Leo to sizzle bacon, but I haven't got the time right now."

After Beeler had got the money, jacket, and six-shooter, she rummaged in the parlor for Nerissa's writing paper. She shook the lavender sachet bag out of the box and hauled out a sheet. Bad luck. It was the wrong box of paper. This was edged in black, the kind of paper a person used to write letters about how sorry he was that somebody had died. Well, it would do in a hurry. Beeler uncorked the ink, grabbed the steel-tip pen, and wrote, making slow scratching sounds. Writing came hard. After all she'd only had two years with the wisdom bringer in Cottonwood. There wasn't time to be elegant anyway—not that she could. But Nerissa would be able to read it. And what she couldn't understand, Elnora could tell her.

She wrote:

Leo Quiney is a horse stealer. He took Jinglebob and went north after Graber. He took J.E.B. Stuart with him, too. I'm going after them to bring them back. I mean—to bring Jinglebob back. I'll see you when I see you. Tell the teacher in Cottonwood that maybe I won't be in school in time. It all depends on how things work out. It may take longer than I have in mind for it to take. But I'll get back—dead or alive. Don't you fret.

Beeler thought of adding "Love" but didn't. And she'd be danged if she'd tack on "Your humble obedient servant" the way the schoolmarm said folks ought to end up a letter. She added only, "Miss Beulah Land Q."

By the time she was half finished with the letter, Elnora was ready with a sack of supplies and utensils. She'd used a white flour sack, but that was all right. She said, "Beeler, I put in a piece of cherry pie and some hoecake and other things, too."

"Like what?"

"Some more bullets for the six-shooter."

"That's fine," said Beeler. "Elnora, where's my critter? I looked for him last night after supper, but he'd moseyed off."

"He's around. I seen him come outa the orchard just after Leo rode off."

The sisters hurried to the corral together. Elnora cornered Two Cents. Beeler quickly put bridle and saddle on him and, with Elnora's help, fastened the supplies and jacket to the saddle. Beeler already had the six-shooter stuck in her belt. When she got up onto Leo's horse, she rose high in the stirrups to look beyond the corral.

"I don't see the critter," she told Elnora.

Elnora was smiling and pointing. "Look beyond the barn. He's there. He's keepin' an eye on things."

Beeler looked toward the barn. There he was, most likely waiting for something special in the way of breakfast. She whistled with two fingers as Elnora stepped back out of the way.

"Are you takin' him along, Beeler?" she called out.

"Uh-huh. He needs to run some of the tallow off him. You tell Nerissa he came along to keep me comp'ny. She won't mind. It'll tickle her to get rid of him."

Beeler watched admiringly as the coal-black, twelve-hundred-pound steer trotted out to her whistle to fall into line behind Two Cents. She grinned with pride to see how the morning sun shone on his sharp curving horns. They were coming along right well now that he was going on three years old. They were growing longer every day and a mighty handsome color, too— a nice dark blue. He was surely turning into a prime longhorn!

"*Adiós*," Beeler called out to Elnora.

Elnora waved as her sister rode north. She cried after her and the longhorn, "Good-bye, Beeler. Good-bye, Travis."

2 TRAVIS

On a hunch Beeler rode to Cottonwood, thinking she might find Jinglebob there. Travis, steer-like, stopped at times to graze in the brush until she whistled him on. Then he came at the swaying trot longhorns were famous for.

But Leo and her horse weren't at the doctor's house, and neither was Graber. They'd both been there together, the doctor's wife told Beeler when she came up to the front door. Beeler didn't ask to visit Parker this time. Instead she asked, "What'd Parker have to say to them two?" She figured the woman would have stuck around to throw Leo out again when he got too rambunctious. She'd most likely heard every word the three of them said.

"Well, dear, the blond boy told Parker he was going north to Lovelock, and your little brother said he aimed to go with him because it was a Quiney duty. Parker told them that he agreed it was the right thing to do, since he couldn't go himself and the family owed it to such a loyal friend."

Beeler grunted. That sounded just like Parker. She said to the woman, "Will you tell Parker that I'm headed north, too?"

The doctor's wife looked shocked. "After those two *boys?* Did Nerissa give both Leo and you permission to go?"

Beeler laughed. "You bet she didn't. He snuck away, Leo did. You tell Parker that piece of news to put in his craw. Leo stole my horse when he lit out after Graber. It's my horse I'm goin' after—not Leo Quiney. Leo can go to Lovelock"—she paused—"or anywhere else he has it in mind to go to. Missus, how long have they been gone?"

"About an hour and a half, I guess."

"*Adiós,* and thanks." Beeler ran back down the steps and out the gate to where Two Cents was chewing on the picket fence. Travis stood ten feet away eating the buds off the rosebushes that stuck up over the pickets. Longhorns didn't mind the company of horses.

"Travis, you keep up with us now," Beeler called to the steer once she'd mounted Leo's horse. "We're gonna heat our axles gettin' outa here."

Beeler dug her heels into Two Cents three times before he gave up fence-post chewing and started to move. She didn't look behind her to see the flabber-

gasted look on the doctor's wife's face. She knew it
would be there. The woman would drive straight out
in her rig to visit Nerissa, spreading the news that
they were all on their way to Lovelock. That was good.
It would save writing a letter later on.

Trailed by her critter, Beeler went straight through
town, now and then tipping her hat to folks she knew.
Nobody called out whoa to her to ask where she was
bound. Cottonwood folks had learned a long time ago
not to mess with Quineys—unless it was Nerissa, who
wasn't one at all except by marriage.

Two Cents did not want to ford the little river
north of Cottonwood, but Beeler forced him over. As
for Travis, two whistles fetched him out into the red-
brown water, splashing across. He'd watched Two
Cents go over. As longhorns went, Beeler knew, Travis
was plenty smart. That was because he'd been around
folks all his life. He wasn't just an ordinary cow brute.

Beeler caught up with her brother at dusk some
thirty miles on the main trail north of Cottonwood.
That was the one she knew he'd take. She would have
sneaked up on him and Graber but for J.E.B. Stuart.
J.E.B. smelled Travis and set up a barking that would
drive a wolf to suicide. There wasn't anything else for
her to do but ride straight on up to the campfire they'd
built.

The boys had tethered the horses and were squatting beside the blaze. Both got up, Leo with the Winchester ready. Nate reached for the one he owned. It was on the ground.

"It's me, Beulah Land, you scrubs," she called out, as J.E.B. ran yapping past her before Travis could kick him.

"For gosh sakes, Leo. It's that sister of yours," she heard Graber say.

"Holy snakes," exploded Leo.

Beeler cried, "I come after you, Leo."

She watched him put the Winchester down and heard him say, "I ain't goin' back with you."

Beeler laughed. "I don't want you to." She pointed toward Jinglebob. "It's him I'm after. I brought you your old Two Cents. You give me back Jinglebob. But first you got to feed me supper and put me up for the night. I ain't ridin' back home in the dark alone."

Leo called out in a fury. "I need a good horse to go to Lovelock. No, you ain't takin' Jinglebob back! He's goin' with me." The boy folded his arms.

Beeler snorted. Leo was acting just the way she thought he would. "You want me to scratch up your wishbone?" She swung out of the saddle. With one hand on the horn and a foot still in the stirrup, though, she suddenly froze. A horrible howling rose up from the mesquite behind her. It sounded very familiar.

It made Leo shout out, "Beeler, did you fetch that critter with ya?"

"I surely did, you son of a goat." She was off Two Cents now.

"What are you two talking about?" Nate demanded.

Leo flung his hat on the ground and jumped on it. "She's fetched that Travis along. And that means J.E.B. Stuart's done for on this trip."

"Done for? Travis?" asked Graber.

"Uh-huh. If there's any one thing a longhorn can't abide it's a dog. J.E.B. is hightailing it for home right now. Dogs don't take kindly to longhorns neither."

"There's a cow out there? A cow came here with you?" Nate sounded surprised.

Beeler whistled. Travis lumbered into sight, hooking his head to the left. His eyes looked red in the firelight. He'd driven J.E.B. off all right—and he wouldn't be back.

"Is *that* what was on the front porch?" Graber sounded awed.

"Yep, it's my poor critter," explained Beeler. "I raised him by hand so he likes me. He was doin' poorly when he was a calf and couldn't keep up with a trail herd passin' through Cottonwood, so one of the herders give him to me because I was handy in town that day."

Leo threw in, "I always say he thinks she's his ma."

"What about my horse?" asked Beeler.

Leo stuck out his chin. "I told you. And I ain't gonna argue with you. Only a fool argues with a female or a mule. I'm keepin' Jinglebob." He turned to Nate. "You're bigger'n she is. After she whips me, I want you to whip her. And you keep Jinglebob for me no matter how beat up I am. I'm goin' to Lovelock with ya."

Graber was astonished. "My Lord, I can't fight a girl, Leo."

"She ain't a girl. I don't rightly know what she is."

Beeler stuck her thumbs into her belt. She wasn't one bit worried about Graber or scared of him. He had the look of a chicken-hearted rooster about him all right. She walked over to the fire and looked at the bacon and can of tomatoes the boys had set out. She thought it might be smart to woo Graber's stomach. "I got cherry pie and hoecake in my sack. I bet that's better'n what you got. I'll share it. Why don't we have some grub now and talk about this in the mornin' when we're feelin' less tindery?"

"You aren't going to beat up on Leo?" Graber didn't look quite so worried now.

"Not right now I ain't. Mebbe later."

Nate smiled. "You'll go back in the morning then?"

Beeler smiled too. "Mebbe I will and mebbe I won't. One thing about you menfolks, you're awful quick to tell womenfolks what to do, ain't you?"

Nate pointed at Travis. "What's he up to?"

She laughed. "How good do you know your Bible, Graber?"

"What do you mean?"

"I'm talkin' about the Book of Ruth. In it Ruth tells old Naomi, 'Where you head out, I'll head out, too.' If Travis hadn't been a bull calf, us Quineys woulda called him Ruth, the way he acts with me."

"Does he obey you, Beulah Land?"

"He comes when I call him—as good as a dog does. He don't do no fancy tricks like sittin' up to beg. But he won't let varmints come around us. Longhorns can be mighty fine lookouts for anybody travelin'."

"They're all loco, plumb demented," muttered Leo.

"Well, I've had a little experience with them. I traveled with a trail herd once." Beeler caught the note of awe of longhorns in Nate's voice. His next words tickled her. "What do you suppose he'd do if somebody tried to make trouble for you?"

The girl took her jackknife out of her pocket and began to saw bacon off the slab into the frying pan set out for supper. "I can't rightly say. It ain't never happened yet, but he appears to dote on me." She shot her brother a look that ought to have made him think twice. "All I can say for sure is that Travis can get in a sod-pawin' frame of mind at times."

Leo spoke up sourly again. "As long as she's around, Nate, we're gonna have this horned jackrabbit of hers with us."

Graber sounded thoughtful. "We haven't got a dog anymore, Leo. I'd depended on J.E.B. Stuart."

Beeler scoffed, "That pot hound."

She woke before dawn, having deliberately put down her blankets on some lumpy ground so she wouldn't sleep heavily. Leo wouldn't steal another march on her! At sunrise Beeler began to sing, loud enough so her brother would hear her:

I slept and dreamed that life was beauty.
I woke and found that life is duty.

Then she said, "Get up, you hog!"

Leo rolled out from under his blankets in a rage. First he put on his hat, then his boots, the proper way to do it.

"Yep, I'm still here with you," she told him, sweet as maple syrup. "And so is my critter, grazin' right over there."

Graber got up yawning. "Good morning, Beulah Land." He put on his boots, next his hat, which proved more than anything else that he wasn't a true-life cowboy. He went to the creek nearby, washed his face, combed his hair, and came back to start the fire.

Beeler rolled up her blankets, went after water for the coffee from the creek, then got what was left of the hoecake out of her sack. She plunked it onto

Graber's tin plates and poured molasses over the cake. It made a jim-dandy breakfast.

After they'd eaten, Leo spoke his piece. It was clear that he'd been pondering during the night, just as she had. "Beeler, I'm goin' with Nate no matter what. And Jinglebob's goin' too. The way I see it, you got to shoot me to get him away from me. You're related to me by blood so I don't think you'd do that. There's only one other thing you can do now. Beat up on me and then get thrashed yourself by Graber."

Nate yelped, "*No!*"

Leo ignored him. "Yep, after you get whipped by him, you'll go back home without Jinglebob anyway because Graber won't let you take him. I'm goin'. Nate's a friend of Parker's. I gotta help him. I'm a hog for duty, remember."

"No!" cried Nate again.

Beeler also ignored him as she sat back on her heels, grinning. She told Leo, "I did some ponderin' too last night. Jinglebob's my horse. Where he goes, I go. It'll suit me just fine to see somethin' of the world other than Cottonwood and Quiney mules and feather dusters. I'm comin' with the two of you. I'll be ridin' Jinglebob and, Leo, you'll be ridin' Two Cents. That's the only way it's gonna be. Otherwise, Graber, you'll have to knuckle scratch with me."

Graber got up so swiftly Beeler could hardly have

believed it for somebody running so much to fat. He
howled, "I can't fight her. Leo, she can't go with us.
She's a girl!"

Beeler gave Nate one glance. "Now don' you fret
over that, Graber. As for me bein' a girl, anything
Leo can do, I can do. Ain't that so, Leo? Just bear it
in mind, Graber, that you came askin' for a Quiney for
comp'ny. You let Leo tag along even when you heard
Nerissa tell you no. Look at it this way. You're gettin'
two Quineys!"

Leo spoke up now. "She can do most anythin' a
Quiney man can do." He said it mournfully, with his
eyes on the three horses.

Beeler laughed. "It is so." She gazed happily at
Jinglebob. Riding him north would be pure pleasure.
She said, "I can help out with the cookin' and the
talkin' when we get to Lovelock. With three of us
askin' around about your pa, you got more chance of
findin' him fast. Besides, with me comin' along, you're
gettin' two valuable animals. There's my critter too."

"Somebody might shoot him on the way," Leo put
in hopefully.

"Not when he trots along right beside Jinglebob."

Nate made a face as he picked up the coffeepot.
"Oh, all right. I'm outnumbered. Even one Quiney
can outnumber most people."

Leo got up. He looked stiff as a fire poker when he

said, "Beulah Land, there's one thing you gotta know first. You have to keep up with us. You better stick or get left behind."

She laughed. "You're gonna be ridin' Two Cents and Graber'll be on Stupid. They're jughead coyotes, them two. You two'll have to keep up with Jinglebob and Travis."

Beeler didn't worry about Nerissa's sending anyone after her and Leo. For one thing, she'd left a letter, and the doctor's nosey wife would spill the rest of the beans. There wasn't anybody at home to send after them—not unless Nerissa called in some older Quiney who'd already left home. And there wasn't much danger in that. None of them could read a letter if he got one.

Traveling on Jinglebob was the pleasure she'd thought it would be. Travis didn't pester him, and he didn't pester Travis. Longhorns surely favored company on the trail. They generally walked with cow-brute partners. A horse wouldn't do as well as another critter for Travis, but a horse was better than lonesomeness. And besides, she was there to talk to the steer and sometimes to sing to him. He'd always cottoned to singing. He seemed to favor hymn tunes.

Leo sulked all the time, trailing her on Two Cents. For a while Graber sulked too, but then after a couple of days he got more friendly. He never exactly jollied her along, but he was plenty polite to her. And she tried to be polite to him. There was a lot to him. He talked elegant some of the time and had refused to fight her. The fact that he was a good camp cook had made her wonder at first until he told her that some of the best cooks in the world were men. But she just couldn't get him to take to Travis. Stupid felt the same way. He wouldn't even come within kicking range of the black steer.

Beeler noticed that the country changed the farther north by west they went. It was getting higher. And the nights were cooler. The post-oak woods got fewer and fewer. There were meadows of tough grass in their place.

Over-the-River was the first town they came to. It was in pretty hilly country with sandy red dirt under-hoof. Over-the-River was a newer town than Cotton-wood was. Anyone could see that, because the saloons were made out of raw wood and the jail didn't have any steps out front yet—just some boards set on nail kegs. Over-the-River had more soldiers in it than Beeler had ever seen before in her life. There were men in blue uniforms wherever she looked up or down the mud street.

"Bluebelly Yankees," she whispered to Leo, who'd come up beside her on Two Cents. Travis was between

them with a rope around his neck. He could tolerate
Two Cents when he had to. Beeler was making sure
nobody'd shoot him.

"How come there's so many bluebellies here?" Leo
asked Nate, once they'd gone through Over-the-River
and camped in a meadow of daisies.

"Camp Concho's nearby. It's an Army post. A couple
of trails go through here, too. Beulah Land, you and
Leo stay here, please, and I'll go back and ask about
my father in town."

Insulted, Leo flared up. "You don't want us along?"

Nate shook his head. "You Quineys were Confed-
erates during the Civil War. The war's over. The
soldiers are U.S. Army soldiers—not bluebellies. They
aren't Union Army Yankees." He sighed. "I'd better
go alone, and you keep that steer here with you."

Leo was miffed. "I want to go. That town's surely
got its hair on."

"It has," agreed Beeler. "It looks plenty rough. And
that's a good reason for *you* to stay clear of it, Leo."

To Beeler's surprise, Graber bowed and swept off
his hat to her before he climbed onto Stupid. "Thank
you, my lady, for your charming cooperation and un-
derstanding."

She stared at him. Nobody had ever done that to
her before. Graber seemed to look a mite thinner.
It was becoming to him. Being on the trail could cut

down some of a person's tallow. "You sure can sling words," she told him admiringly.

Nate came back just before dark. He had more supplies with him, more bacon and flour, but no news. "Nobody's seen five men riding together," he told the Quineys as he sat down to "poor do," Beeler's supper of bacon drippings, canned tomatoes, and biscuit crumbs.

As Beeler poured Nate some coffee, she said, "That ain't so strange. Who'd take notice of five galoots ridin' along together?"

Nate put down his cup. "Just about anybody might. These five men aren't ordinary. My father looks like me. His hair's blond and curly. He used to be rather portly."

"What about the other four?" Beeler asked.

"One of them's very big and broad. Another's very small—smaller than most women. One's fat enough to be in a circus, and the other's a real beanpole."

Leo whistled. "I guess you'd notice them all right. Is that what the Mexicans told you?"

"Yes, all of those men—my father, too—worked in the silver mines down near Santa Inez."

Beeler was curious. "How come they left Mexico?"

"I was told it was dangerous working there because of Mexican bandits. The bandits hung around waiting to rob the Mexican miners' payroll when the cash came from the nearest Mexican city. Maybe bandits ran my father and the other Americans out." Nate shook his head as he picked up his cup. "The Mexicans in Santa Inez only mentioned bandits once. When I asked for more information, they wouldn't talk about them anymore. They did mention the payroll and the bandits together, though."

Beeler had finished eating by now. She said, "Mebbe the bandits ain't Mexicans. Mebbe they're the men we're lookin' for. Mebbe they got a payroll and lit out over the border with it."

Nate's face got turkey red. "Are you trying to tell me that my father's a criminal? He was a schoolteacher by profession."

Beeler said, "That ain't exactly what I'm sayin'. What I'm sayin' is that mebbe your pa knew they took the payroll money, and they knew it. They'd shoot him or take him along with 'em to keep him quiet, wouldn't they? It's what I'd do."

"You'd shoot him," came from Leo.

"Oh, hush up, Leo."

"Yes, please be quiet, Leo," came from Nate, who was looking into the campfire. Finally he turned his head to stare at the girl. "You know, Beulah Land, that makes some sense. My father wouldn't have left Santa Inez of his own free will—not if he'd written to me where he was. If your idea's right, he's a prisoner. You're pretty smart, aren't you?"

Leo scoffed. "Smart—but not pretty."

Beeler sniffed. She asked Nate, "Are there other towns between here and Lovelock?"

"Yes, Comanche Springs. That's what they told me when I asked south of Cottonwood."

The country just north of Over-the-River impressed Beeler, though the two boys didn't seem much interested in it. She'd never seen so many wild flowers in her life. They bloomed in patches—yellow, red, purple, pink, and blue. They made her think of a crazy quilt. Quilts could be mighty pretty things. She didn't much take to housecleaning, but she could still find looking at some of the things in a house pleasurable. That's what it was like in this part of Texas in mid-June—a big bright bed under a bright blue ceiling. Jinglebob pranced under her while Travis lagged behind sampling a mouthful of this and that flower. She didn't for a minute blame him. If she'd been a critter, she'd have tried a taste or two of each blossom, swaying so prettily in the wind.

Now and then, being polite, Beeler would turn in the saddle and look behind her. Her brother and Graber were keeping up right smartly, but then Jinglebob wasn't setting much of a pace for their coyote horses.

Comanche Springs wasn't much different from Over-the-River except that there weren't any bluebelly soldiers there. There were men in this new town in blue overalls building a railroad, laying rails. The cowboys riding into Over-the-River had fist fights with the soldiers, while those who came to Comanche Springs had railroad gangs to knuckle scratch with.

Stupid and the Quiney animals didn't like the new tracks, slim and shining in the sunlight, one bit. They had to be led over, one by one, while they snorted and stomped, unwilling to touch a rail with a hoof.

Beeler wasn't surprised when Nate left her and Leo outside town once more and rode back alone. He returned with the same report as before: no news. "I guess we'd better go on to Lovelock then," he said unhappily. "Nobody saw them. I asked about my father and the other men in every saloon in town, all twenty-three of them."

"Was your pa a old whiskey soak? Does he like scamper juice?" asked Beeler.

"No!" She thought Nate seemed put out by the question. He added after thinking for a minute, "At least he didn't use to drink at all."

"Folks do change," she told him with a nod. It was something the schoolmarm in Cottonwood kept on saying. It wasn't a Quiney saying. Quineys said "Folks start out wicked and generally get worse the older they get."

The more she pondered it, the more Beeler grew sure of Nate's pa being mixed up in something funny. But she wouldn't worry him about it. He wasn't made of the same stuff Quineys were. He hadn't let out one cuss word on the trail. Every morning he'd been polite, even when Stupid flopped down and tried to roll in the sand by a creek before he could be saddled. And he slicked up too. Sometimes when there wasn't a creek or pond handy, he used drinking water from his canteen. He even had a toothbrush along. It gave Beeler a sinking feeling to watch him using it. She'd plumb forgot to bring hers along.

No two ways about it, Graber was a gent, an elegant one! She was almost sorry they'd have to part company with him in Lovelock. She'd learned one or two things already from keeping an eye on him. Because she'd been around him a good bit, she could even put on elegant airs sometimes when she wanted to now. Elegant airs might come in handy someday when she was away from Quineys. They weren't the only folks in the world! Traveling had taught her that.

But there was no teaching Leo anything. He was as ornery as ever. One thing about him—he wouldn't ever learn from his betters because he wouldn't ever admit he had any betters.

A couple more miles on the trail took them and Travis to high plains country. The wind blew hard here. Grass bent under it while trees grew runty, queer, and twisty. Large birds rode the sky over the riders.

"They're eagles," Nate said, tilting back his head to look at them.

"Eagles are better'n buzzards," was Leo's only comment.

Beeler didn't say anything. She didn't like this country. There weren't any sounds in it but the wind and sometimes the cry of coyotes. They made the horses and Travis nervous. She talked to Jinglebob and the steer at the same time, keeping Travis close on his neck rope. It was lonesome, and it was sad for all of them.

She hoped Lovelock wouldn't be sad, too. But something inside her said it might and they'd get news there they wouldn't like. She dropped back once to talk to Leo while Nate was trying to get Stupid up out of the bottom of a gulch they'd slid down into by accident.

"Do you think Graber'll find his pa in Lovelock?" she asked her brother.

Leo answered right off after he jerked Two Cents' reins, stopping him from biting Jinglebob on the neck. "Nope. It appears to me that if his pa came this way with them other four, somebody woulda taken notice of those five funny-lookin' galoots."

"You bet they would," Beeler said thoughtfully.

Then she asked, "What do you think old Nate'll do if he can't find him there?"

"Go back homesteadin'. And you and me, we'll go back home."

"What's beyond Lovelock? You talked with Graber last night. I didn't. Your bedroll was right by his."

"Deadahead, more'n seventy miles away."

"And what's on the other side of there?"

"Texas stops after Deadahead, and New Mexico Territory begins."

Beeler was thoughtful. "Leo, we never traveled out of Texas, did we, except to the mule market in Missouri? Far as I know, no Quiney ever did."

Leo agreed. "I never heard tell of a Quiney who did, but there's some of the boys we lost track of. No Quiney we know anything about has ever been much of a wanderer. And if anyone ever did leave Texas, it would have to be a man from our kinfolks. New Mexico Territory surely ain't for females."

Beeler snorted. "Just how come it ain't, Leo?"

"Graber told me somewhat about it last night. It's supposed to be full of desperate characters from all over, some of 'em even from Texas. It ain't no place for puny, weakly womenfolks."

For the second time Beulah Land snorted.

3 TURNIPS AND CARROTS!

One thing pleased Beeler about the land near Lovelock—there were some little lakes around. A person could take off her boots and soak her feet while she took her leisure in the shade of a willow tree. The horses could drink up. Travis could wander around in the shallow water, bellowing and snorting, or just stand chest deep, looking off into the distance thinking whatever longhorns thought.

But they couldn't dillydally too long by the water, because Nate's pa could be moving on ahead of them, too, going to this Sundown or Sunset, that nobody had ever heard of in either Over-the-River or Comanche Springs.

Lovelock turned out to be a surprise. It was bone-dry. There wasn't a single saloon in the whole town. Nate, who'd traveled more than either of the Quineys, said he could hardly believe it. The three of them stood in front of the Nicodemus Hotel with Travis tied between Two Cents and Jinglebob, staring at the

people of the town. They were mighty rough lookers
—long-haired and dirty and dressed, more often than
not, in buckskin instead of cloth.

Nate told Beeler and Leo quietly, "There are some
buffalo hunters here, and I think some buffalo-bone
gatherers, too."

"How do you know for sure?" asked Beeler.

Nate sniffed. "You can smell a buffalo hunter half a
mile away."

Beeler snuffled too. There *was* a stink in the air. It
smelled the way it did when pigs were slaughtered
back home. That was a time of year she didn't like
one bit. She asked Nate, "With there bein' no saloons
here, where'll we ask about your pa and them men?"

"Cafés and the hotel and stores, I guess."

She nodded. "This time I'm lookin' too. Leo," she
ordered, "you ride herd on my critter and the horses.
Graber'll take one side of the street and I'll take the
other."

Leo burst out, "I can ask, too!"

"No, I'm a faster talker than you are. The next
place we go, you can mebbe ask Graber to let you help
him hunt in saloons."

"Beeler, I sure wish you'd stayed to home. I'd sure
like to get rid of ya."

She laughed up at him. "You didn't think I ever felt
welcome with you, did ya?"

She tethered Jinglebob to the hitching post, then

put Travis next to him. Nate secured Stupid, leaving Leo still mounted, watching over everything, but scowling.

Beeler took the right side of the one-street town, Nate the left. She went first of all into the hotel. No, five men answering the travelers' descriptions weren't staying there and never had been.

Next she tried the Fair Deal Chop House between a livery stable and a ladies' dry-goods store—not that she'd seen any women in Lovelock yet. But there was one at the café, an oldish one, wiping off the oilcloth on the tables. Nobody else was in sight because it was eleven o'clock. What the old lady wiped off— crumbs, steak bones, and all—went down onto the sawdust floor. It wasn't much of a hash house, Beeler decided.

"What can I do for you, young man?" she asked Beeler.

"I ain't," said Beeler.

"You ain't what?" The woman straightened up.

"A he."

"No, on second look you prob'ly ain't. You got braids, though, and lotsa boys around here got them. Is your pa or ma here? It's too early for grub to be served up. What're you doin' here? You ain't alone, are you, girlie?"

"No, I ain't alone. Have you seen five men travelin' all in a bunch?"

The old lady smiled. "Lotsa times, dear. Them buffalo hunters and wild-horse catchers that come here for eats, they go around together. They surely shovel in the grub—prob'ly because this year they can't spend their money in saloons. Mebbe next year the mayor'll say there can be whiskey again."

Beeler sighed. This was taking too much time. She described the five men as Nate had described them. The old lady looked at the ceiling, thinking and humming. Then she nodded. "Yes, sir, I did. But it was more'n a month ago—more like two months. My memory ain't so clear no more. But I think it was when my son and me just opened for bus'ness. They was like that—tall and short and fat and skinny, but the number five man was bald. He didn' have no yeller curls. His forehead went all the way over and ended at the back of his neck."

Beeler frowned. "Did he have blue eyes?" Nate's were blue, like the color of bluebonnet flowers.

"Oh, dearie, mosta the time I'm too busy to take notice of things like that."

"Ain't there anything else you can remember, Missus?"

The woman tapped her foot and hummed some more. Then she smiled, showing teeth that were mighty fine, too fine to be hers, Beeler decided. "Yep, there surely was. The bald man was mighty polite to me. That made him stand out."

"His kid's polite, too. That'd be him," Beeler cried out. "Where were they headed?"

"Lordy, I don't know, honey. They didn't settle around these parts. I never saw 'em agin in Lovelock."

"Didn't they say at all where they were going?"

Once more the old woman pondered. She sighed, then told Beeler, "Deep down in my gizzard I seem to recall that the bald-headed one said somethin' about restin' from a long ride when he got to where the sun sets." She wiped her hands on her hips. "That's right. And the big one told him to quit jawin' about it with me because they had to hit the trail right away to get the most miles they could outa daylight."

Beeler wanted to know, "Have you ever heard of a town called Sunset or Sundown?"

"No, girlie, but I can tell you somebody who might know."

"Who'd that be?"

"The postmaster of Lovelock, that's who. He come here last week. You'll find him in Barger's Store, where the buffalo hunters get their supplies."

"Much obliged." The girl gave the old lady a swift grin and ran out of the café down along the rutty street to where a glum Leo waited. "I found the galoots," she shouted at him. "They came through here!"

"Where are they now?"

"On their way to Sundown or Sunset—if they ain't already there. We're gonna find out where that is right away." Beeler untied Jinglebob and Travis and mounted. She whistled her Travis whistle. It made the steer jump and start moving, but it did something else, too. It brought Nate bursting out of a store from across the way. He came pounding over, raising up more dust in the street.

"I thought your steer had got loose, Beulah Land."

"Nope, I was callin' you, Nate." Quickly she told him her news and saw hopefulness spread over his face. He mounted Stupid as quickly as he could, though the horse tried to lie down in the street the minute he got his boot into the stirrup.

Barger's Store was a big place, plumb full of men buying this and that and smelling all the way up to heaven—buffalo hunters for danged sure. They made way for Beeler, more out of surprise at seeing a girl in pants than anything else, she decided later. She marched right up to the iron bars that had *Post Office* painted on a sign above them. In a place like Lovelock it was pretty clear to her why the postmaster might want to stay in a cage. It could be safer than out in the store. Buffalo hunters appeared to be mean-eyed as well as stinking of buffalo blood and buffalo fat.

Because it was Nate's pa they were hunting, Beeler let him do the asking. But she stood right behind him with her hand on the butt of the six-shooter in her belt. Men were crowded up all around them both, curious to know what they'd have to say to the postmaster. Would he have a letter for them? She guessed there weren't many folks in Lovelock who'd get letters —let alone be able to write them.

Graber said to the postmaster, "Please, sir, is there a town anywhere at all around here called Sunset or Sundown?"

The postmaster shook his head. "No Sunset or Sundown that I know of right offhand, my boy, but let me look in my book for one."

"Have you got a whole book of just towns?" Beeler asked, very impressed.

"I sure have, young man."

This time Beeler didn't correct him. The way the buffalo hunters were laughing, the postmaster could be told about it later on. Instead she called out, "Thank ya."

She watched while the man turned the pages of a largish book. He soon closed it and looked up through his ugly little steel-rimmed spectacles. "I take it by 'around here' you refer to the State of Texas?"

"Yes sir, or hereabouts," said Nate.

"Texas? Or *hereabouts*?" The postmaster took off his spectacles. "Well, Uncle Sam's book of U.S. towns with post offices in them says there's a Sunman in Indiana, a Sunflower in Missouri, a Sunbury in Ohio and in Pennsylvania, and a Sun Prairie in Wisconsin. Nothing at all in Texas—at least not at the moment."

"What about the territories west of here?" Beeler cried out over Graber's shoulder.

The man chuckled. "I looked under the territories also. Nothing. But that doesn't mean much, given them."

"How come?"

"Because the communities west of here are often like mushrooms. They pop up overnight and disappear a month later. Uncle Sam's post-office system can't catch up with them. Many of them are mining towns. You know, here today and gone tomorrow."

Nate asked, "You think if there is a Sundown or Sunset, it's west of here?"

The postmaster brought his lips together, put on his spectacles again, and nodded. "Probably, if there is such a place."

"Is that your cow-sense opinion for sure?" asked Beeler.

"Young man, there is no 'for sure' when it concerns anything about New Mexico Territory—or for that matter, Arizona Territory. I'm going on common sense. I am not a cow. The sun sets in the west. You've noted that the states east of here don't have such a town. I should think logic would tell you that this town lies in the far West."

Beeler jabbed Nate in the ribs with her elbow and

hissed into his ear, "Who's this here logic? Mebbe he'd know."

"It isn't a he," Nate whispered back. He said to the postmaster, "Thank you very much."

Outside, away from the throng of buffalo hunters, Beeler drew in a noseful of clear air. Nate was looking at his boots, mighty down in the mouth. "Buck up," she told him, feeling sorry for him. "They rode through here, them men, on their way to the same place you heard of in Old Mexico, didn't they?" She'd decided not to ask about logic.

Graber turned up the toes of his boots sadly. "But *where* is it?"

Being friendly, she hit him on the shoulder with her fist. "West of here, that's what logic says. We'll find it."

He shook his head. "No, it isn't right. All I ever asked was for somebody to go to Lovelock with me. I'll go back to the homestead now."

"You're gonna quit huntin'?" Beeler put all of her scorn into her voice and words.

He looked properly stung. "You mean you and Leo will go on with me? We'll need more supplies."

"Sure we will, Nate. You buy what we have to have here." She hauled her egg money out of her pants pocket and held it out to him.

Suspiciously Nate looked first at Leo, guarding Travis and the horses, then at Beeler. His eyes narrowed. "You're hoping to get out of school by going with me, aren't you, Beulah Land?"

She scoffed, "Not me. Leo is for sure. I don't mind school so much. But it can wait. This way I might be seein' somethin' of the world I'd otherwise never get to see. I been ponderin' while we rode along. It ain't so easy for girls to traipse all over as it is for boys. Girls get stuck at home all the time."

He chewed this over and finally nodded. "All right then." He looked more cheerful around the jowls, Beeler decided. And he took the money. "After all, this town we're looking for might be just over the very next hill."

Beeler looked over the flat prairie. There weren't any hills in sight at all. "Well, mebbe at the bottom of the next big dry gulch and not on the map yet. Ya know," she added, "it's a Quiney duty to help you out all the way to wherever you're goin'."

Graber shivered a bit, even though it was plenty hot in the sunshine of June. "Please don't tell me ever again that you Quineys are hogs for duty."

"A hog, or a pig for that matter, ain't a stupid animal, no matter what folks say. Me and Leo, we took to ya. We like you. Get more grub, and we'll get on our way west to Deadahead. We can do some askin' there, too."

Two Cents tried to kick Beeler as she came up to

Leo, but she dodged his hind hooves the way she always did. "Leo," she said, "we're goin' on with Graber."

He gave her a fish-eyed look. "You and me, Beeler? Both of us?"

"Sure. Graber's buyin' more supplies for us right now." She patted Travis on the muzzle. He'd been mighty well-mannered in Lovelock among so many bad-smelling people.

"Where are we headed, Beeler?"

She swung her arm in a wide gesture toward the west. "Over there. That's where this here place has got to be. The postmaster told us so."

She waited until Nate returned with a sack of supplies and mounted up, too. Then Leo put in, "While you two was in town bein' so all-fired important, I was askin' some questions of my own out here."

"What did you find out?" asked Nate.

"There's a Army trail through here. It runs from Camp Concho, down by Over-the-River, to Fort Sumner in New Mexico Territory. If your pa and them others went into the Territory, they most likely traveled on it, too."

Beeler said happily, "I bet that's so, Leo. It's a good thing them five look so peculiar, ain't it—bald-headed, too! You can't miss spottin' him, that pa of Nate's. More'n likely them five dropped their names in the river if they headed into the Territory."

Graber knew what she meant all right. "There you go again, Beulah Land! Listen here, you don't know one thing for sure about them. You've got it all set up in your head that my father's changed his name because he's in trouble with the law. Next thing you'll say is that you expect to find them hanging from a tree somewhere."

"One thing you can say about old Beeler, she likes to be right, no matter what she says," Leo told Nate, as he gave Travis's neck rope to his sister.

At the same time Beeler noticed that he gave her a funny little smile. She thought it was the kind of grin he'd given her once when he put a burr under Jinglebob's saddle back home just before she mounted. Elnora had seen him do it and tattled on him, so Beeler had scratched his wishbone up plenty that time. It was the same grin all right. Sort of mean and tight. Seeing it didn't give a body a lot of comfort.

Leo looked to have something up his sleeve. Beeler held onto Travis's rope until they'd gone a mile or so from Lovelock. Then she took it off him and dug her heels into Jinglebob's flanks. The horse spurted ahead of the other two, with the longhorn moving smartly alongside him.

She told Jinglebob and Travis as soon as they were out of earshot of her brother and Nate, "Leo is up to devilment. We got to watch out for him. But whatever he's got in mind, it ain't gonna work!"

They trotted into Deadahead in the late afternoon. It was a dugout town, made of houses with their innards dug out underground and with their roofs covered with grassy sod. Several of the houses had flowers growing on the rooftops. Travis paid them some heed as they went through town and hitched their horses to a rail set out in front of one of the only two wooden buildings in sight, a general store. The other one next door was a saloon.

Nate decided they'd try the store before they tried the saloon. Once more they left Leo on guard while they started to ask around. The store man was short, with billygoat whiskers. His wife was taller than he was and some younger, with sharp little blue eyes, yellow curls, and a very fancy gray dress, with a bustle, trimmed in white curlicue braid. Beeler guessed she wore paint. Her cheeks were a wicked-looking color.

Mr. Billygoat Whiskers nodded when Nate asked about the five men. "Yes, sir, me and Elfie, we sold 'em supplies last month, didn' we, honey gal? Or was it month before last?"

Elfie smiled at him as if she truly favored him. "We surely did, a whole fifty dollars' worth." She gave Beeler an odd, questioning look, which Beeler knew by now meant, "Are you a boy or a girl?"

"I ain't a he," said Beeler. Suddenly she asked before Graber could get in his question about Sundown or Sunset. "What'd they pay you folks in? American gold pieces or Mexican silver pesos?"

The whiskery man blinked. "Mexican money. Anything that's hard money is good in these parts."

"Ah hah!" Beeler told Nate.

"Ah hah, what?" He turned his back on her, letting her know she wasn't going to get a rise out of him, though it ought to be clear as sin to him. If the men used Mexican money, they sure could be bandits.

"Where were they headed, ma'am?" he asked the woman storekeeper.

"I don't know. We were very busy that day trying to outfit some men bound for the mines in New Mexico Territory." She gestured toward a stack of pickaxes and shovels against a wall.

Nate asked, "Did they buy mining supplies?"

"No, sonny," came from the man. "I'd have remembered that. Only grub and ammunition."

Nate looked a bit worried now, Beeler thought. He asked, "Were *all* of them carrying guns?"

"To the best of my memory they were, sonny."

"Even the bald-headed galoot?" asked Beeler.

The woman chuckled. "I think he must have been, or else I'd have taken note that he wasn't. Most menfolks do hereabouts. It's fit and proper for *men*." She cast a very disapproving look at the six-shooter in

Beeler's belt. "He had such fine manners. He even took off his hat to me when I measured out pints of speckled beans for him. That's when I saw he had no hair to speak of."

"Bald as a boiled egg is how I heard it in Lovelock," volunteered Beeler.

"Are you looking for those men?" Mr. Billywhiskers wanted to know.

"We sure are," said Nate. "I think I'm the bald one's son."

"Don't you know?" Elfie sounded surprised.

"I haven't seen him in a long time," Nate explained. "He had curly hair last time I saw him."

"Well," remarked the woman, "it could be that he has lost it all by now. Time has a way of making tracks on a lady's face and on a man's scalp." She asked, "Will you be wanting supplies too?"

"A pounda coffee beans—if you got 'em already roasted," said Beeler.

As the woman picked up a scoop to take the beans from a big jar on the counter, Nate asked her husband, "Do you think they traveled west?"

"It would appear so. There's nothing north of here or east of here. If you've traveled the military road from Lovelock, you'd have met them going south. Flat as this country is, it'd be hard to miss five riders."

"Thank you for your information," said Nate, paying for the bag of coffee beans.

"How many of you are there?" Elfie asked Nate.

"Three of us and something that belongs to her."
Nate jerked his head toward Beeler.

"Something?" The man looked puzzled.

Beeler explained. "My critter. Come on out and
see him."

The couple followed her and Nate out to the edge
of the porch where Leo, the horses, and Travis
waited. "There's my animal." Beeler pointed to the
steer. It seemed to her he wasn't getting much thinner
for all the trotting around he'd been doing. Traveling
was mighty becoming to him. His hide was as slippery
and shiny-looking as black satin.

"He's our watchdog," said Graber.

"Always on the job," boasted Beeler, "and never
barking at the moon like some fool hound."

"No, he only unnerves my horse and me by prowl-
ing around half the night stepping on dry sticks in the
mesquite," complained Nate.

To Beeler's surprise, Leo took off his hat to the
woman. The sun shone on the redness of his hair.
"Howdy," he told the couple.

The woman nodded and nudged her husband. "Just
look at him. Such a darling little boy!"

Beeler was stunned. Leo, that runt, darling?

"Do you suppose he'd like a big piece of pound cake
and raspberry shrub cooler? He looks spindly," said
Elfie Billywhiskers.

"He probably would," agreed Nate.

"I surely would." Leo was already off Two Cents, tethering him.

Beeler stood waiting beside Travis, expecting to be included in the grub invitation. She noticed that Nate was waiting, too, jiggling the sack of coffee beans. But only Leo got "invited." He sashayed past Beeler, smirking, holding his hat over his breast. When he was beyond her, he turned and said, "You ride herd on things for a spell, ya hear?"

Mr. Billygoat Whiskers ignored her, too. He turned to Nate. "Do you want to have a look at the new map I've got of New Mexico Territory?"

Nate grinned now. He shoved the sack of coffee beans off onto Beeler and trotted beside the man into the store again. Beeler plunked herself down on the porch, opened the sack, and took out a coffee bean. She started to chew on it. It was bitter as gall. No, she didn't like Deadahead. Nate would probably go from map looking to cake eating. Her eye fell on a sod house across the way. The grass beside it was green and high. The flowers on its roof were yellowish-white, the very color of pound cake. She got up and untied the steer, leaving his neck rope dangling. Maybe he could get some pleasure out of grazing, and she could get some out of watching him.

For a long time she sat on the porch in the fading

sunlight, now and then yelling at Two Cents when he put back his ears to take a hunk out of Jinglebob. When he stuck his neck way out, that Two Cents looked just like a snake. He was a trial to everybody. Nobody came near Beeler while she watched the horses. Nobody seemed to be at home in Deadahead—or maybe the houses had been deserted because folks moved on. Maybe they'd all lit out for New Mexico Territory too!

Finally Beeler heard footsteps from behind her on the porch. Elfie Billywhiskers was there smiling, a piece of cake in her hand in a napkin. "The sweet boy said you might like some, too."

Beeler shrugged. "I ain't partial to pound cake." She turned her back.

But that didn't stop the woman. "How about that handsome animal of yours? Wouldn't he like a carrot or a turnip?"

For a fact, Travis doted on root vegetables. Beeler got up again. Why make things hard for him? "Sure, he favors 'em just fine."

Elfie smiled again. "Go behind the store, dear, to the root cellar. I opened the door already. The turnip bin's in the far right corner. Take some turnips and a carrot too."

"Much obliged." Beeler walked around the side of the house, found the open door in the ground and the flight of steps under it. She went down them into the dark coolness of the cellar where these folks stored their root vegetables. Because it was underground, it had an underground smell. She could just make out the turnip bin. She took two turnips and started back when all at once the door came slamming shut over her head.

A big turnip in each hand, Beeler stood in the dark listening to Elfie Billywhiskers calling to her from outside the door.

"Don't you try to shoot your way out. You can't. I've bolted the door already. Our root cellar will hold even a dangerous lunatic like you. It's where you'll be until the doctor comes from Lovelock. Your little cousin has told me all about you, Bertha Mae Muller!"

4 MR. McCARTY

Beeler threw both turnips hard as she could at the closed door of the root cellar. She ducked one boomeranging back but got hit on the knee by the other so hard that it made her fall down. She pulled herself up, went up to the door as near as she could, and pushed on it. Elfie had shut it tight—just as she said. It wouldn't budge one bit.

Beeler turned her back on it and sat down on the bottom step. "Hang and rattle, Beulah Land. How're you gonna get outa here?" She repeated fiercely, "Hang and rattle! Quit fightin' your head."

She put her head in her hands, muttering furiously. But slowly the muttering stopped, and she scrooched around to look at the door again. Cracks of light showed only at the edges. The door appeared solid enough for coffinwood. Beeler went up to it and pushed some more, not that she was very hopeful. For sure it was locked from the outside—bolted and with a padlock on it by now too. Shooting at it wouldn't be worth a hoot, though it would surely attract some attention.

She sat down again. Attracting attention by hollering, shooting, and shouting wouldn't do a mite of good. Deadahead wasn't a Quiney town. Nobody would stand up for her here. That's what the Elfie female expected, for her to kick up a big fuss that would make people believe she was loco.

"What was the name she called me?" Beeler suddenly asked herself. "Bertha Mae Muller!" That was the name of the yellow-headed girl in Cottonwood Leo was half stuck on. Leo! *Cousin!* Sure as shooting, it was coming clear now to Beeler. Leo was behind this whole thing. Only she and Leo would know who Bertha Mae Muller was. Nate wouldn't.

"Why would Leo say he was my cousin and tell that big lie about me?" Beeler wondered. The answer came even more quickly than the name Muller had. To get hold of Jinglebob and to keep her from traveling with him and Nate. The look she'd seen on his face back in Lovelock ought to have made her wary of him. She'd guessed he was up to something, but she just hadn't been wary enough.

Her thoughts went to Graber. She pondered for a while, then decided that he wouldn't be party to her being clapped into a root cellar. But he'd go on traveling with Leo and leave her behind all right. Leo was smarter than she'd given him credit for. He would cook up a story that'd convince Graber fast. Graber hadn't wanted her along in the first place. They'd surely plan to leave her here in Texas. Probably until they came through Deadahead on the way back and picked her up. Or maybe they figured the doctor from Lovelock would send her back to Nerissa with some travelers going that way.

"Cuss that Leo!" Beeler suddenly exploded, banging her hand on her knee. It hurt, making her think of Jinglebob, which hurt too. Leo would take him, of course. He might just leave Two Cents behind for her but probably not. For certain Leo would take her supplies.

She laughed suddenly in the dark brown gloom. At least, Leo wouldn't be taking Travis. Travis had never cottoned to him. The critter was loose, even if he had a rope around his neck. Anybody but her who tried to mess with him would learn fast what he was dealing with. Travis! Beeler started to worry about him. Would he get into trouble? Maybe Deadahead folks didn't fancy having their roofs chewed on by long-horns. Maybe somebody would shoot him as a public pest. Nate wouldn't let that happen, if he could stop it, but what if he'd already lit out with Leo? After the dirty deed Leo had done, he wouldn't be likely to stay around in Deadahead. He'd want to put some distance between him and her.

Her mind went back to her critter. He wouldn't be getting his turnips. All at once she got up to examine the door once again. The light coming through the cracks was fading. It was getting on to dusk. That was good. There wouldn't be a moon until later on. A black critter in a dark night. That was just fine!

She'd wait. Because she was hungry she felt around in the root cellar until she found the potatoes and carrots. She helped herself to a raw potato and, after she'd finished it, stuffed two big long carrots into her back pocket because they were skinnier than turnips and more comfortable. When she guessed it was dark enough, Beeler got as close as she could to the side of the door where the daylight had shown widest. She put her fingers into her mouth and whistled loud as she could—so loud that it hurt her ears. She waited a bit and whistled some more.

She didn't have to whistle more than six times. While she was getting ready to pucker and blow for the seventh time, she heard a whuffling sound from the other side of the door. He'd hung around the way she guessed he would. Travis was there outside, being curious. When he made that kind of sound it proved that he was.

"I'm down in here," she called out.

A thud answered her. The steer had pawed the

door. Beeler laughed as the thudding got louder.
Travis hated doors. Doors kept him out of the Quiney
house where he always wanted to go. He hated front
porches almost as much because Nerissa wouldn't permit him to sleep on hers. Because the root-cellar door
was nearly flat with the ground, Travis would be
bound to think it was a front porch, too.

Beeler called out again, "Travis, I have to get out
of here. I've got some carrots for you."

The thumping got wilder now. The door shook
while dirt rolled down from the sides into the cellar.
Beeler knew an instant later from the rattling and
crashing that the longhorn was standing on the door
trying to hook the crossbar with a horn. She surely
hoped he wouldn't fall through and get stuck.

She moved farther back into the root cellar out of
the way. The strong door held. It was the ground on
the left side of it that gave way, tumbling down the
steps in a rush of clods of earth. Beeler didn't delay a
blessed minute. She pushed up through the dust and
squeezed out beside the door, though she had to shove
the curious steer's muzzle away because he was blocking her escape.

Beeler was out and on her feet just in time to grab
his neck rope before Mr. Billywhiskers came out onto
his back porch with a lantern. Behind him came his
wife with a shotgun.

"Where'd they go?" yelled Beeler. "Where'd that

runty cuss of a brother, who calls hisself a cousin, and that fat curly-headed kid ride off to?"

"You get back down in that cellar," cried the woman.

Beeler stuck out her tongue. "You can't make me do it. My animal'll kick down your entire emporium if I tell him to."

"I can shoot him," said the woman.

Beeler leaped in front of Travis. "Then you got to shoot me, too."

"Elfie," pleaded the man, "you mustn't shoot the child—even if she is a dangerous lunatic. What would folks think about us if you did?"

Mrs. Billywhiskers lowered the shotgun. "Are you going back down there, Bertha Mae?"

"No, I ain't. And I ain't no Bertha Mae Muller neither. Did Leo Quiney travel west? He's my brother."

The man looked at his wife. "He did, some time past."

"And you, you old mossback, you saw him take all the horses with him. The bay horse belongs to me."

Elfie had a cackling laugh. "They got all the horses with them. That'll hold you here, whoever you are. You can go back down there in the cellar or be locked up in the store until the doctor's come. You must be a lunatic, travelin' with two boys. It isn't fit and proper. Well, you can't trail after them pestering them anymore, can you?"

Beeler glanced at Travis, who was snorting because he didn't like lanterns and hollering folks. She sighed, then told him, "Just remember, Travis, it won't be for very long." She led him to a nail keg beside the house, got up on it, and flung a leg over his back. The longhorn snorted some more and pawed around a bit, then let Beeler neck rein him away from the back porch.

"Much obliged for the cake and carrots and all your hospitality," she called back over her shoulder, as they headed past the root cellar for the street.

Travis swayed along in the ruts past the store. By the time they were abreast of the one saloon, curious folks were coming up out of their sod houses across from it. If Travis hadn't made noise enough at the root cellar, Mr. Billywhiskers and his rouged-up wife surely had. There'd been some uproar!

Beeler waved to the folks of Deadahead. It was going to be nice saying *adiós* to them. To one galoot standing on the steps of the saloon she even took off her hat and said "Good evenin', Mister." She paused to ask him, "Which trail's the soldiers' road to New Mexico Territory?"

He pointed north by west. Even if his mouth was wide open, he didn't say a single word. Beeler watched him shiver once. Then he turned in a circle and went right back through the swinging doors fast as he could.

"Thank you kindly," she called after him, as she

and Travis left Deadahead. Under her breath she told the steer, "I never could stand the looks of a old whiskey soak. He sure hightailed it back into that saloon fast as he could. He was hardly polite at all."

Several miles outside of Deadahead Beeler slowed Travis to a stop by jerking on his rope and saying "whoa." She'd ridden him often enough when he was a calf for him to know that when she pulled up on the rope she had it in mind for him to stop so she could slide off. He wasn't any Jinglebob. Riding Jinglebob, even bareback, was the next thing to sitting in a rocking chair back home. Bareback on Travis resembled trying to get comfortable on a sawhorse more than anything else. Longhorns were pretty much what folks in Texas called them: "A pair of horns with a steer hitched underneath them." Travis's spread wasn't quite four feet wide yet, but he'd have a respectable five feet pretty soon. And from then on there was no guessing how long those handsome blue horns would be.

Proud of him and of herself, too, Beeler pulled the carrots out of her pocket by moonlight and gave them to him, one by one. She talked to him. "You did real fine back there, critter. I'm sure glad them folks didn't take after you with Winchesters for eatin' the flowers off their roofs. Mebbe they wanted somethin' to come along to keep the green growth down. Mebbe you did 'em a service." She patted him on the muzzle, then leaned against him to look northwest while he chomped carrots.

She'd already seen the point of fire way off in the distance. A campfire for sure. That was where Leo and Nate most likely were—out of Texas and into New Mexico Territory. They were danged certain she wouldn't be following them. Well, let them count their chickens before they hatched. With a half moon to help her keep Travis on the trail, even though there were some clouds out at times to drift over it, she ought to be on top of them by midnight. And aboard the big longhorn she didn't have to be afraid of coyotes or wolves. They'd shy off from him.

Flinging her arm around the steer's neck, Beeler told him, "And then, Travis, all hell's gonna bust loose." A minute later she hauled herself up onto him once more and said, "Rattle your hocks outa here."

Because it was hard to tell just how far away a campfire was, it took Beeler longer to get to it than she'd expected. She came up as quietly as she could and stood staring at the fire, still a goodly piece away. Her eyes were mighty sharp. She could pick out Graber in his Mexican hat and that runty Leo real good, but there was somebody else with them.

He was wearing a black hat. His horse was there,

too, hobbled not far from the camp. It was a big gray. But the stranger wasn't fussing over it. He'd brought Jinglebob up near the blaze and was petting him.

Beeler put wrinkles between her eyebrows pondering. She'd planned to come crashing right up onto Leo, threaten him with a chasing from Travis, then jump off and beat the stuffing out of the no-good son of a goat backstabber. Then she'd give old Graber a good piece of her mind. But with somebody else there, it might not be the best thing to do. She might get shot, and more than likely her critter would.

"You stay out here, Travis," she told him softly, as she got down. "When I whistle, you come on in."

Beeler had been told more than once by Nerissa that she had a voice like a rusty gate hinge. But it was a girl's voice all the same. As loud as she could, she started to sing as she walked forward, "Jesus Loves Me." That would do double duty—to let them know she was loose again and on her way up to them and calm the longhorn, being left alone for a while. He loved that tune. When Nerissa played it on the cottage organ, he'd sneak up and stand under the big pecan, enjoying it.

It satisfied Beeler's thirst for revenge to watch Leo jump up and Graber too. It wasn't quite so pleasurable to see the stranger drop Jinglebob's halter and draw out a pistol. He carried a hogleg on his hip. Beeler buttoned her jacket over the six-shooter in her belt and went on singing as Nate called out something to the stranger. She guessed Graber must be telling him they knew who it was, but the stranger didn't put down the pistol.

"It's me, Leo. It's me," Beeler called out. Then she went on with the hymn again and sang it until she almost reached the campfire.

By this time she was glad to see that the stranger had put the hogleg back. Taking off her hat, Beeler stepped into the firelight. She said howdy to the stranger while she gave him a quick look. He wasn't too old yet, probably around twenty or so, but he was getting on. He was so thin he wouldn't make a meal for a yearling tomcat. He wore old pants and boots and a black handkerchief at his neck. His hair under the black hat was shoulder-length and yellow colored. He wasn't a buffalo hunter. There wasn't any smell to him at all.

Beeler gave her real attention to her brother. "Yep, it's me, old Bertha Mae Muller, you runt. You got snake's blood, havin' that Elfie Billywhiskers lock me in the root cellar. Well, it didn't work. I'm back, and I'm ready to scrap with ya."

"How'd you get outa there?" Leo demanded. "She said that cellar'd hold you."

"Root cellars won't hold me when my temper's fiery

and my feelings tindery, you son of a goat horse thief, Leo Quiney. You're the worst brother a girl ever got saddled with."

"Muller? Quiney?" Beeler heard the stranger's soft voice as he turned his head toward Leo.

Leo sank down beside the fire. "We're both Quineys, her and me. She's my sister."

"Your sister was out on the prairie all by her lonesome, *walkin'*?" asked the stranger.

Beeler felt she might warm to him for saying such kind words. She told him, "I wasn't plumb afoot but the next thing to it. I've got my critter with me. I'm gonna whistle him in now, Mister . . . ?"

"Henry McCarty, ma'am."

Beeler had a smile for him and for his politeness. "I'm Beulah Land Quiney. We're from Santa Rosa County, Texas. You know my runt of a brother and Jonathan Graber here. They talked a woman in Deadahead into lockin' me in a root cellar as a dangerous lunatic." She gave Nate a toothy grin of triumph. He was looking mighty red in the face, the way he ought to look. "Ain't that the truth of it, you fat scrub?"

Graber suddenly blazed up. "No, it isn't! Leo told me you had the chickenpox and the woman had put you to bed until the doctor came from Lovelock. Leo and I planned to pick you up again when we came back."

"Sure, sure. And you waited for me to get unsick like a real gent, didn't you? And you took my horse. Well now you know what Leo really did to get rid of me because he wanted Jinglebob." She turned away from Leo and Nate to point to her horse. "Mr. Mc-Carty, that is my animal. The coyotes belong to them two. Keep your hogleg where it belongs, and you'll meet my other animal."

She whistled. Seconds later Travis, red-eyed in the firelight, hove into view, his horns glistening.

McCarty laughed. "Well, look at the brush splitter. Did you ride him here from Deadahead?"

"I surely did. He goes where I go. He lets me ride him when I want to. Where are you from?" Beeler had decided that she wouldn't hit Leo right now. She'd be polite, too. She'd wait until the stranger had gone.

"Just about anywhere in New Mexico Territory. I been all over."

"Where are your folks?"

He didn't say anything for a minute, then he re-plied, "My pa and ma are dead. I got a brother in Silverado. That's all."

Beeler said, "It's the same with us Quineys. We're leppies, too. But I got plenty of brothers. Most of 'em, I'm glad to say, are better'n him." She nodded toward Leo. "Mr. McCarty, did Graber tell you about his pa bein' missin'?"

"He sure did. He asked me about Sundown or Sunset, but I never heard of it—though there's a Puerto del Luna just north of here."

"That means 'port of the moon,'" said Nate unhappily. "It has to be the wrong place."

After she'd watched Travis mosey off to graze, Beeler went up next to the fire, took Leo's cup, and poured herself some coffee. "Are you gonna hunt for Sundown with us, Mr. McCarty?"

"No, I'm stayin' in this part of the country."

Beeler watched McCarty squat down beside the blaze. He surely had little feet and hands, not much bigger than hers. He pulled two little white rocks from his pocket and nervously began to toss them from one hand to another. His eyes never kept on any one thing for more than a couple of blinks. They were light eyes, bluish, set off more by the sunburned brown of his face. Beeler looked over the rim of the tin cup at McCarty's belt. He wore his hogleg low, even if it was a common .41 six-shooter. It surely had a tiny little handle. Cowboys mostly had pistols, but McCarty, she had the feeling, wasn't any more a cowboy than he was a buffalo hunter.

She spoke to Leo. "I ain't gonna forgive you. I'm gonna keep a eye on you from now on all the way to Sundown. The first trouble you give me you'll be missin' your best bridle teeth." Next she spoke to Nate.

"Mebbe I'll forgive you, but you was mighty quick to believe a cock-and-bull story you coulda checked out pretty easy."

Leo muttered, "I ain't gonna fight with ya, Beeler. It'd be useless as barkin' at a knot."

"That it would, runt. I'd win—like always." Beeler turned to McCarty and asked sweetly, "Have you seen much of Texas, Mister?"

"I been to El Paso a couple times, ma'am. Mexican gals there smoke *cigarillos*. Have you ever tried one?" He pulled out a long black thing from his vest pocket and offered it to her.

Beeler looked at the *cigarillo*. She'd always hankered to try a cigar but hadn't. She'd had a chew of tobacco, though, turned green, and been sick for two days on it. Maybe *cigarillos* did that, too.

"Thank ya, no. I ain't a Mexican." She didn't feel so warm toward him now. Tempting her with tobacco!

He laughed. "That's too bad. They taste mighty fine." He struck a match on the sole of his boot and lit the *cigarillo*. "Let me gave you a piece of advice. You ain't in Texas now. There are lotsa Mexicans here, and they ain't got no love for *Tejanos*. Step polite-like here."

"We don't have it in mind to pester any Mexicans," Beeler protested. "Nate talks Spanish real good."

McCarty looked solemnly at Nate. "That's good. You better do the talkin' around Mexicans then."

"I will. Thank you for the warning, sir."

" 'Sir,' " McCarty laughed again. Now he threw away the rocks, took the pistol from its holster, and began to turn it easily on one finger of his right hand, cocking it as it went over. Beeler sat down across the fire from him and watched, fascinated by the skill of his hand. Leo watched too. McCarty saw their interest, smiled, transferred the six-shooter to his left hand, and did the same thing. It wasn't as if he had it in mind to fire it. He was playing with it, thought Beeler, the way somebody would play with a pretty-colored lizard.

Finally Leo exploded admiringly, "Holy snakes, you can do that just as good with one hand as the other one! What else can you do with it?"

"Well, I can put all six bullets in a tree while my horse gallops past it. I can put two pistols on the ground, and when you toss up two empty tin cans, I can grab the hoglegs and bust open both cans while they're still up in the air."

Beeler spoke up hastily. "We ain't got nothin' but Winchesters with us, Graber's and Leo's."

"But, Beeler," started Leo. "You got a . . ."

"Sure," the girl interrupted him. "I *had* a six-shooter, but old Mrs. Billywhiskers took it away from me in Deadahead."

Leo sounded amazed. "How'd she do that?"

"By holdin' a shotgun on me. How else?" Beeler told a second lie. She gave McCarty a sidelong glance. He wasn't an ordinary cowboy. The easy way he played with the pistol made her feel chilly all over. It was a "play-pretty" to him, the way a doll was to a weaner gal. She'd keep her jacket buttoned no matter how hot it got as long as they were with him. Henry McCarty made her jumpy.

It didn't ease matters one bit later to have him start to talk in his soft voice about the haunted waterhole he'd visited in south Texas. The ghost of a pale woman with a baby in her arms walked around it at midnight. He'd seen her. Beeler hoped Mr. McCarty would keep his promise and not travel with them.

Suddenly she became aware that he was talking to her, "How come a little gal like you is on this here errand, too, ma'am?"

Beeler chose her words carefully. "More'n likely Leo didn't tell you he stole my horse. He did it twice, so he's a two-time horse thief. I'm only followin' the horse and seein' that he's took care of. I used to care about Graber's locatin' his pa until he did me that dirty trick back in Deadahead along with Leo."

McCarty sounded melancholy. "You know, that's just about all I ever did care about myself, ma'am. Horses and my only brother and a little Mexican gal in Fort Sumner—and a Englishman once who was mighty good to me."

"I never laid eyes on a Englishman," said Beeler. "But I'd surely like to see what one looks like. I'd like to go to England where they all come from before I get bogged down in carpets the way most girls do back home."

"Mebbe you'll be that lucky. I never been to England. I don't think I'm gonna get there either." McCarty put the six-shooter into its holster, got up, and stretched. He said to Nate, "Thanks for the good grub. I'll ride with ya a ways tomorrow and see that you're on the right trail."

"We'd all appreciate that, sir," Nate said politely.

Beeler watched McCarty go over to his bedroll. What she'd appreciate would be his leaving right now. He hadn't even twitched when she'd told him Leo was a horse stealer twice over. That more than likely meant McCarty was too. She'd spied her bedroll lying beside Jinglebob's saddle on the ground a few feet away. She wouldn't have to sleep on a Tucson bed, the bare ground, tonight. But it wouldn't be restful having a six-shooter poking her in the ribs all night.

Henry McCarty left them at noon the next day. At breakfast she'd spied the pink scars on both of his skinny wrists. He'd had sheriff's irons on him, and not long past either. She had whispered to Nate as they saddled up Stupid—who generally needed two people, one to hold his head, the other to get his saddle on his back—"Be careful, Graber. I think mebbe McCarty's a wanted man."

Out of the corner of his mouth Nate had told her, "You better stop whispering to me. He's looking at us."

Beeler had watched their night visitor ride north and, when he was out of sight beyond a swell in the land, had breathed easier. After that they followed the soldiers' trail he'd marked out for them, and no one said a single word about him, which was odd.

The country had changed since they'd crossed over into New Mexico Territory. It wasn't green prairie anymore. It was higher and rolling. The land was green-gray and tan, and there were bluish mountains ahead, the first real mountains the Quineys had ever seen.

Sometime after they'd parted company with McCarty, they saw two horsebackers coming from the west. Beeler opened her jacket while Leo got one Winchester ready and Nate the other. The riders, both men, were old roosters this time. One was gray-headed and had a face shriveled by the sun. The other one was wide-faced with a dark mustache that drooped over his mouth, covering it up.

He was the one who asked, "What the devil are you sprouts doin' out here in the wilds?"

"Looking for Sundown," answered Nate. Then he explained about his father.

"I never heard tell of such a place," said the man with the mustache, "but I wish you good luck lookin' for it. My name's John Poe. I'm huntin' somethin' too—a boy not much older'n you." He stuck out a finger at Nate. "He's got yellow hair and blue eyes . . . name of William Bonney."

Nate answered, "We were with a Henry McCarty last night, sir, no one named Bonney, though he did have yellow hair."

Poe had a very sharp laugh to him. "McCarty will do. So will the Antrim Kid. Most folks call him Billy. He's wanted for murder as well as horse theft. He's killed a lot of men hereabouts. He's mighty nervous. You're lucky you're all right. Where was he headed?"

Beeler shivered, thinking how, bold as brass, she'd come to the fire last night and whistled Travis in too. McCarty might have turned his hogleg on all of them. That would have given him Jinglebob, the other horses, and their supplies. But he hadn't taken anything more than a plate of beans and bacon.

"What direction was he headed?" asked Poe.

Leo spoke up right off. He'd surely admired McCarty. "South!"

Nate didn't say until Poe looked at him. Then he stared at the ground and said, "East—sort of."

Beeler glared at the two boys. What liars! No wonder Nerissa got mad at men for sticking together. "No sir, Mr. Poe. McCarty, or whoever he is, rode north!"

The gray-haired man started to chuckle, then said, "We know that he didn't ride west or we'd 'a seen him, Poe. Somebody here's a Texas flannelmouth. I bet it's the fat kid and the redheaded filly. Sprouts like that little bitty one over there ain't got the horse sense yet to tell lies. We'll ride south the way he says to."

After the two men had ridden past them going south, Beeler spoke scornfully. "Texas flannelmouth liars! That's the pair of you. How'd you ever tie up with a wanted man in the first place? I thought it wouldn't be smart to ask you last night in front of McCarty—or whoever it was."

The answer came from Nate. "He came up to us out of the dark and asked if he could share our fire. He was polite as could be. I felt sorry for him. He looked hungry and ragged."

Beeler nodded. "I took note of that too."

"Like his pockets were plumb empty of jingle," volunteered Leo.

Nate went on. "He told us that he could read and write."

This made Beeler sigh and glare at her brother

again. Outlaws could read and write! Leo couldn't yet.

Leo ignored her, saying, "Ya know, I think he was plain lonesome, and we wasn't anybody who'd be bothersome to him."

Beeler looked north where McCarty had ridden alone. She nodded. That was her opinion too. She said, "High lonesome, more'n likely. I guess that's what happens to men the law wants. Let it be a lesson to ya, Leo."

5 MARVELOUS MELINDA

The three Texans didn't talk again about Henry McCarty. Beeler knew why. Thinking about him made her mournful. But that wasn't all that did. The country up ahead didn't comfort her. She grew more and more awed by the mountains stabbing to the western sky. Santa Rosa County had hills, but nothing that could be called mountains. These must be as big as those mountains in Switzerland that the schoolmarm had shown stereopticon slides of once. Just looking at them had made Beeler feel like a wart on a big pickle. These mountains did the same thing to her. She guessed Leo felt sort of the same way. He kept glancing behind him to see the familiar flatness of the prairie, then ahead of him with a queer, doubtful look on his face.

Nate didn't seem so disturbed. He'd seen mountains before in Old Mexico. Mountains meant mines to him, he told Beeler and Leo once when they halted the horses. Mining was something his father knew a lot about, and he might be prospecting for gold or silver. People in the next town they came to might know if there was a mining town named Sunset or Sundown in these mountains.

While Beeler listened to him, she kept her eyes on his face. She was pondering Graber all right. He had some sand in him and seemed to know what he was about, but she still wondered about what had gone on back in Deadahead. He or Leo had better never try any more dirty tricks on her. But she had to admit that she didn't feel exactly easy about things without them either. They were out of Texas now. Down in her gizzard she knew that she'd made a big step. By leaving Texas she'd thrown in her lot with them— Jinglebob's and Travis's, too. The fact didn't sit well on her mind, but she wasn't about to let the boys know. Those two were thicker than feathers in a goose-hair pillow.

It seemed to her that they rode quite a ways before they came to a place they never even learned the name of. It wasn't anything more than a trading post for antelope hides. One thing this country was full of was antelope. Antelope liver cooked up just fine for supper.

The long-bearded man at the trading post wasn't any help at all when it came to knowing about Sundown. He'd never heard of it and had no idea where it could be. Sociableness was in his character, though— either that or he was lonesome. He told them that they'd gotten off the trail to Fort Sumner and were southwest of it. He thought now that they'd done that, they might be smart to travel along in that direction toward Silverado, where he'd heard lots of folks traveling out of Texas were headed. That was the big mining town in the Territory. He added that fifty miles west of his trading post they'd get their feet wet crossing a river named the Pecos, and it would be wise of them to join up with some other travelers going the same way just as soon they could.

"It's Indian country down there. You got to keep a eye peeled for Apaches," were his last words to them. "It's hard to figure Apache Indians. Sometimes they let you go by without your ever seein' 'em. Sometimes not. Watch your horses good. Apaches like mule and horsemeat better'n they like beef."

Beeler patted Jinglebob's flank. No Apache would get him! "How about grass for the horses and my critter up ahead?"

"You'll find some, even if the grazin' ain't as good as it was in Texas."

As Beeler started southwest, away from the mountains on Jinglebob with Travis by her side, she found herself almost wishing McCarty was riding with them.

He'd said he had a brother in Silverado. That meant
he knew the way there, and she was more than sure he
knew how to get on with Apaches.

The Pecos wasn't much more than a brook and easy
to ford. A couple of miles farther west Beeler and
the boys were pleased to see three riders coming. Winchesters and six-shooter ready, the Texans waited. The
horsebackers were men once more, but this time they
didn't ask about McCarty. The biggest, fattest one,
almost redheaded enough to be a Quiney, called out,
"Who'd ya be? And what're ya doin' out here?"

After she whistled Travis next to her, Beeler called
out, "Come on in, and we'll talk." She kept her hand
on her belt.

One of the riders laughed. "Ah, they ain't nothin'
but kid colts!"

The horsebackers came in closer, riding around the
Texans, giving them the once-over. But it was Travis
they mostly stared at. Travis accommodated them by
snorting and turning around so they could admire him
from every side. Beeler was proud of his handsome-
ness. Finally the redheaded man said, "Is this here
animal you folks' steer?"

"He ain't theirs. He belongs to *me*," said Beeler.
"He's got our brand on him, a letter *Q* with a barbed
tail on it. That means Quiney down in Santa Rosa
County, Texas."

"It don't mean nothin' here," came from the third cowboy. "We're from the Chisum Ranch. All this country's Chisum land from Fort Sumner to the Texas line."

"And there ain't no welcome mat out for settlers or squatters," said the redhead.

"We aren't settlers. We're only passing through, sir." Nate told his story and asked his question.

The redhead pushed back his hat. "I never heard of any Sundown, kid, but that don't mean much. You better go to Ross and ask there. It's a tradin' post." He laughed and pointed at Travis, who was facing him, being curious. "How come you got that big cactus boomer with ya? You figure he'll come in handy for ready beef on the trail?"

Beeler sizzled. "I'd eat you first—hooves, horns, and tail!"

She couldn't miss Nate's sigh, it was so loud. "Put it this way, sir. The steer is a child's pet."

This made all three Chisum cowboys laugh. The redhead called out before they rode off, "You colts are holdin' too loose a rein on that carrottop heifer. You watch out or she'll be wearin' the bell in your outfit."

"She already is," Beeler heard Leo muttering, as he tried to manage Two Cents, who had it in his cranium to follow the riders.

A mile or so farther on, Beeler told both boys in

her most scornful manner, "In any outfit the one person who ain't a horse thief ought to be wearin' the bell and be the boss!"

The traders at Ross weren't any help either, though they invited the Quineys and Nate to "set and eat a bean" with them. The traders, all members of the same family, warned them that Apache country lay due southwest. The Indians hadn't given any trouble for a while, but a place to be careful of them was thirty miles ahead on Ramada Hill. Six miles beyond the hill was the town of Ramada where they ought to be safe. They'd be smart all the same to hook up with some other travelers. Maybe if they were lucky they might be able to find the circus that had been in Ross just the week before.

Beeler saw Nate's jaw drop and watched him stare around at the tiny trading post and deserted country as if he didn't believe his ears. He didn't look much different when he heard that the circus had got lost on its way from a silver town up north to another mining camp.

"A whole circus got *lost?*" Nate asked.

The head trader laughed. "Well, stranded's more like it. They didn't make no money here. Somebody up north said we was a town of five hundred folks— not just fifteen of us. We headed 'em toward Silverado. There's a heap of folks there now, if you can believe anythin' anybody says about this Territory."

"And they went west to Apache country?" Beeler wanted to know.

The traders all grinned at the same time. Because they were related they grinned the same way, with a gap between their two front teeth. "Oh, we didn't guess the Apaches would bother them much," said the head trader again.

"Are they a big outfit?" asked Leo.

"No, they ain't. But they got them animals with 'em. It ain't them common ordinary camels of theirs. The Apaches seen camels by now because there've been camels runnin' loose ever since the U.S. Army brought 'em out here during the War. It's them other beasts."

"What're they?" Leo got the words out before Beeler could.

"Them other critters they got. Them things that look like oversize panthers. One of 'em's got hair growin' all over his shoulders. It's a awful sight. They cough a lot at night."

Beeler heard Graber's quick intake of breath. Even Stupid heard it and shifted from one forefoot to the other. "You mean they have honest-to-goodness lions? African lions?"

The head trader replied, "I dunno where they hail from, but they don't come out of any hills around here."

Nate turned to the Quineys. "They're the sort of

animals that ate the Christian martyrs back in the days of ancient Rome."

"That's it," came from one of the trader's sons. "The man who corrals them brutes calls hisself Daniel. He told me the Bible talks about lions and a Daniel."

"Lions ate Christians later on. Daniel's too early in the Bible, but all the same he certainly does have a lot to do with lions. They refused to eat him," Nate corrected the boy. He spoke next to Beeler, "I've always had an ambition to look at a real lion."

Beeler thought a minute, then replied softly, "Sure, you would, you scrub. You want to see the animals that chewed up the Christian saints all right. You ain't the only one who knows about them. I heard about 'em in Sunday School once. You're plenty wicked, aren't ya, Graber? I'd rather see the poor Christians than the lions that ate 'em. Chew that over."

Nate spoke severely. "It's educational to look at lions, Beulah Land. The Lord knows if there's anything a Quiney needs, it's education. Besides it's not as if these lions are the same animals that ate the Christians."

"They're outa the same tribe, ain't they?" Beeler gave Travis a worried glance. Every mile he went he looked handsomer. Running all over Texas had taken a bit of tallow off him but only enough to put him in prime condition. She asked Nate, "What else do lions eat except folks?"

She'd never noticed what an ornery grin he could put on. "Meat. Just about any kind, I suppose—I think they prefer beef."

That night, because of Apaches, they didn't light a fire and ate a cold supper. They were climbing by now. There were more mountains ahead to the west. And it was getting colder at night because of the increasing altitude. Beeler shivered in her blankets, wishing she could curl up with Travis the way a person could with a warm dog or cat. You couldn't do that with a long-horn, no matter how friendly. But Travis was a good watcher, always on the job. When he heard noises he started bellowing like a lost calf in high grass. But mostly he bellowed at coyotes that yapped all night long anyway.

Beeler was still mighty uneasy. It wasn't so much that this strange country was unfriendly. It was just nobody's country. It made her feel even friendly to-ward Leo at times. Not that she could see that it made him feel that way toward her, but he didn't give her that mean smile anymore so she guessed he wasn't planning anything. Bad as he was, he wouldn't leave her afoot out here where there was nobody for miles around.

Ramada Hill was a steep one. They led the horses up it and down it, Winchesters ready, glancing from side to side. But there didn't seem to be anything to be scared of in the ocotillo bushes and cactus on top. The bottom of the hill was even bushier, full of mesquite and hackberry trees. Beyond them was a line of cottonwoods and more mesquite, which meant only one thing—water. By the way the trees grew, it was most likely a river.

"Be careful of Indians now," Beeler whispered to Nate, as she mounted Jinglebob again, being sure to hang tight to Travis's neck rope.

"Beulah Land, I'm being careful. If we run into any Apaches, please keep quiet. I'll try to talk to them in Spanish."

"Why that lingo?"

"Because the Spanish and the Mexicans were here a long time before Americans came. Apaches ought to speak Spanish if they speak anything except Apache."

Beeler grunted, "Mebbe so. I'll oblige ya to keep the peace."

Leo led the way now on Two Cents with the Winchester in one hand. They'd learned along the trail that Leo was the better shot of the two boys. Nate followed behind, and Beeler brought up the rear with Travis's neck rope fastened to the saddlehorn so she could get to her pistol if she had to.

They heard the queer sound the minute they got out of the brush beyond the hill. It was a sort of grumbling rumbling. For a minute Beeler thought it must be the river up ahead or maybe even a waterfall. But the noise of a river over rocks wasn't a thing that stopped and started.

"Is that Apaches?" she asked Nate.

"Indians don't make that kind of noise. I don't think anything I ever heard did." He smiled all at once. "I think it just has to be lions!"

"From where?" demanded Leo.

"Over there by the river, I'll bet." Nate stood up in his stirrups and shouted, "Hey, is there anybody there down by the river?"

There wasn't any answer, but a very unusual thing happened. Out from under some sagging cottonwoods a contraption suddenly appeared. It glittered in the sunshine. Only the front half of a wagon, it had just two wheels. Two black horses wearing a red harness pulled it over the ground toward them. Most astonishing of all, a lady in a purple dress and purple bonnet with white plumes on its top was driving the queer rig. And it was coming fast.

Jinglebob, who'd never seen such a sight, reared up while Travis tried to jerk away. Two Cents had one look at the wild contraption, turned around on his hind legs, and galloped back toward the hill taking

Leo with him. Stupid held his ground, probably because he was so winded from going up the hill.

"Yoo-hoo," cried the woman driver.

"What is it?" Beeler yelled at Nate.

"It's only a chariot," he called back.

Beeler managed to calm Jinglebob down and to whistle once to Travis, who was plenty wild-eyed and jumpy by the time the lady in the chariot was up to them. Now Beeler saw that each black horse had a white silk banner over his back with printing on it. She read it out loud, even if some of the words were mighty big.

CLAYTON'S CIRCUS
Dauntless Daniel, Tamer of Wild Beasts
and
Marvelous Melinda, Bicyclienne
Camels   Performing Jugglers   Charlie and Blossom

The lady in the chariot pulled up next to Nate. Beeler got a good look at her. She was handsome as a heifer knee-deep in red clover, with dark hair and dark eyes, all purple velvet, white feathers, and white lace—and wearing white gloves. Her voice was velvety, too. "I'm Miss Melinda Holcomb, Bicyclienne, dear," she told Nate.

"I'm Jonathan Graber, ma'am." He lifted his hat.

"This is Beulah Land Quiney, and that's Leo Quiney
back there on the runaway horse."

Miss Holcomb giggled. "I hope I didn't scare you
just now. I was practicing driving the team. I always
go first into a town, you know, ahead of the circus
wagon. It's good advertising. So few people in the
Territory have seen chariots."

Nate was gallant. "You didn't scare us, ma'am. It's
just that our horses haven't ever seen a chariot either."

Because it didn't appear that Nate was going to get
around to it, Beeler asked, "Can we ride to Ramada
with you, ma'am?"

"If Mr. Clayton says so, and I'm quite sure he will,
you may." Miss Holcomb drove up beside Beeler now
to look at Jinglebob and Travis. She smiled and said,
"A commendable bit of horseflesh and cowflesh you
have there, young man."

"I'm a she. Beulah Land's a she-name."

Miss Holcomb's black eyebrows arched higher up.
"A girl traveling with menfolks?"

"My brother and Graber and me—we're on a errand,
all of us. A errand of duty. All us Quineys are hogs
for duty. And a girl ought to help out, too, shouldn't
she, when it comes to duty? Howdy!" Satisfied with her
noble speech, Beeler stuck out her hand and shook the
white kidskin glove up and down. The lady smelled
up to the skies of lilacs in bloom.

"Duty is ever commendable. Come along, my dears." She touched the blacks lightly with a long, gilded whip, making them move forward, then turning them about. They were mighty well-trained, thought Beeler. The woman led the way toward the riverbank with her chariot bouncing around over the bumps in the ground. It didn't strike Beeler as the best way to travel.

"What's a bicyclienne?" the girl asked Nate, coming abreast of him and Stupid as they followed.

"A lady bicycle rider, I suppose."

"I never set eyes on a bicycle, but I saw a picture of one in a *McGuffey Reader*, Nate."

Nate laughed. "I had one when I was little. I fell off it and cut my lip, and I've kept away from them ever since." He glanced over his shoulder at the same time Beeler glanced over hers. Leo had Two Cents turned in the right direction by now and was coming back. Beeler wondered if Two Cents, Jinglebob, and Travis were so emotional about chariots how they would act around bicycles and lions, something else they'd never seen.

The circus wagons were camped beside the river called the Hondo. But it wasn't the river that took Beeler's eye. It was the lions. There they were, two of them, bigger than any cat she'd ever heard of, each in his separate cage. One had brown-yellow hair all over its shoulders—not a bad-looking color, thought Beeler, contrasting it in her mind with her own hair. It was a sort of hairy blond critter. The other one, the one without a mane, resembled a great big yellow female cat. She was licking a paw while the first one was staring straight ahead with eyes like yellow marbles. Both lions turned their heads lazily to stare at the horses, the steer, and the newcomers who were people. For a fact, lions weren't bothered by horses. They yawned, both of them.

Beyond the caged lions were three camels tethered to a red-wheeled wagon. They gave the lady in the chariot and the Texans and their animals a bored look, too.

Beeler spotted some ordinary brown horses tied to cottonwoods and two other wagons. The back of one wagon was open. As Beeler rode by it, muttering to both Travis and Jinglebob to keep them from acting up some more, she took a quick look inside. This wagon was full of shiny metal things, mostly wheels, big and little. Miss Melinda's bicycles, she guessed.

And now a very tall man came walking up from the river, carrying a bucket in each hand, going toward one of the two tents under the trees. He only glanced at the chariot, but when he saw Beeler and the others, he put the buckets down and came forward. He was handsome, too, with blue eyes and whitening hair. He had on red pants with a blue stripe down each side and a blue coat with gold braid and fringe on the shoulders. Duded up that way, Beeler figured he might be Dauntless Daniel, who tamed wild beasts.

Miss Holcomb waved at him. "Oh, Mr. Clayton, the children want to go to Ramada with us."

The circus man walked up, looked over Nate, Beeler, the horses, and Travis, then shook his head. "There isn't any attraction here, Melinda. Longhorn steers don't draw crowds—maybe back in Boston, Mass., but not out here."

Nate put in fast, "We don't have it in mind to be part of your circus, Mister. All we want to do is go through the mountains and Apache country with you. We've got our own supplies. It won't cost you anything. We're worried about Indians."

Clayton laughed. "Apaches haven't even bothered us." He motioned toward the lions' cages. "It's my guess Indians don't know what to make of Blossom and Charlie, so they only peek at us as we go by."

"Would you sic your lions on Apaches, Mister?" asked Beeler.

Beeler saw a look of pain cross Clayton's face. "Those valuable animals chasing Apache Indians! Lord forbid. They're my finest attraction."

Beeler heard someone sniffing and looked over her shoulder. It was Miss Melinda. But Clayton didn't pay her any heed. He didn't even seem to hear her when she said, "Lions. Lions! Your finest attraction! That's all I hear all day—you bragging about those lions. The lions make unpleasant noises all night long, and they smell. It's enough to drive a lady to. . . ." Suddenly she turned to Beeler and said, "It's enough to drive a lady to the company of other ladies." She smiled. "You'll live with me in my tent while we go to Silverado. *I* say you can travel *all the way* with us. That's my tent over there, the biggest one. The smallest one belongs to him. When it rains, he lets the lions sleep in there with him." She sniffed once more, swung the chariot around and bounced away.

Nate asked, "Mr. Clayton, have you ever heard of a town called Sunset or Sundown?"

Clayton shook his head, "No, boy. I never played it in my life. I remember every town I ever played. I pride myself on my memory."

By now Leo was in the circus camp, even if Two Cents was snorting and dancing. Jinglebob was trembling. Beeler couldn't decide if it was the chariot or camels or lions bothering the horses. Miss Melinda had been right about the lions. Lions had a powerful smell to them all right.

"We'll help you work however we can," Nate told Clayton.

"Maybe you can drive a wagon. I'm shorthanded

just now. Two of my workers left when we were up north. The other three went on into Ramada to get things ready for tonight's show."

Just then the lion with all the hair on him let out a cough, and all four of Two Cents' hooves left the ground at the same time. Travis leaped sideways.

"You'd better dismount," the circus man warned Nate. "You seem to be making Charlie nervous with your noise and jumping around."

Beeler glanced at the cage. The lion with the mane didn't look one bit nervous. He had got up and was stretching and yawning just like a huge pussycat. She tethered Jinglebob and Travis to trees beside the Hondo where there was grass. Then she walked to the biggest tent. Tents were queer things. There weren't any doors to knock on, so she yoo-hooed the way the bicyclienne had. "Yoo-hoo," was an elegant expression, Beeler thought.

"Come right on in," said the lady's voice.

Miss Melinda's tent had half the comforts of home. She had a blue rug and a brass bed. There was a mirror hanging from the tent pole. The only thing missing were pictures and mottoes on the walls. But that would be expecting too much for a tent.

The lady charioteer was on her knees opening a trunk. She said, "Mr. Clayton will unharness the chariot horses for me." She flung something out of the trunk onto the bed. It was lavender colored and sparkly. "That's what I'll wear tonight. When I ride the unicycle with Blossom."

"That's one of the lions, isn't it?"

"Oh, yes."

Beeler felt silly. All the same she asked, "Does the lion ride a bicycle, too?"

Miss Melinda's laugh sounded the way water glasses ring when you hit them with something. "Of course not. Blossom trots along beside me on a leash. She is reasonably civilized, though she did bite a Sunday school teacher up north when, the woman got too close to her."

This made Beeler nod. She'd surely tell Nate about that. Still after Christians!

Miss Melinda threw something else out of the trunk, more lavender cloth. "How do you like my costume? Here's the rest of it."

Beeler picked up the two things. One looked like the bottom half of long underwear with feet in it. The other was a sort of corset and corset cover all in one piece. It had black spangles sewed around the neck and purple-and-black cloth flowers, too. There weren't any sleeves at all. It was surely the most naked-looking thing she'd ever seen.

"Holy snakes, ma'am, you don't plan wearin' this in public, do ya? Folks'll see your legs!"

Miss Melinda giggled as she got up. She was looking Beeler up and down. "Well, my dear, aren't you showing your legs in those boy's trousers?"

Beeler dropped the costume onto the bed. "That's diff'runt. I'm travelin' and ridin' a horse astride."

"Well, you could have a sidesaddle, couldn't you, and wear a skirt? I am riding a bicycle. Can I do that in a skirt and bustle? Don't you see my point?"

She flopped down onto the bed and sighed. "Ramada! It will always be the same, I just know it. I'd have all sorts of beaux in Ramada if we'd stay long enough. They'd send me mash notes and five-dollar gold pieces with holes drilled in them for me to wear around my neck. Half of the eligible men in a town always fall in love with circus ladies who wear spangles and tights. Do sit down, dear."

Beeler sat down on the bedspread beside her, hoping her dirty pants wouldn't leave marks on it. She tried hard to be polite. "It must be a trial to have so many beaux in love with you. I never had even one."

Miss Melinda looked glum. "Generally it's very gratifying. But it just breaks a lady's heart when she can't get the one she really is after."

"Who'd that be?"

"Dauntless Daniel Duckworth. That's his real name, you know. But who ever heard of a lion tamer called Duckworth! So he says he's Daniel Clayton."

Beeler nodded. She'd figured Daniel and Clayton were the same man. It didn't seem likely anyone else would sleep with lions in his tent. The lady patted Beeler's hand. "My dear, there is nothing in the world half so painful to the heart as unrequited love."

Beeler took off her hat. "Yes, ma'am. I guess so, but my sister-in-law, Nerissa, back home in Santa Rosa County says having it requited is worse sometimes. She says livin' with all of us and with my oldest brother is like wearin' a mustard plaster both front and back."

Miss Melinda pulled some fancywork out of a tapestry bag under a bed pillow. "Tell me about you, dear. What's this errand you're on?'

Beeler told her. The lady had tears dropping from her eyes when she heard of Nate's pa being missing and stamped her foot, mad as all get-out, when she heard about Beeler's being locked in the root cellar. She vowed that Travis must be the finest and most intelligent longhorn in Texas. He ought to be able to learn tricks easy as pie and in no time at all be a circus performer too.

Beeler was tickled to hear Travis praised. "My critter is the smartest one in the whole state—and my cuss of a brother's the most sneaky, ma'am."

The bicyclienne snorted. "He's getting in practice to be a man, isn't he? Look at Mr. Clayton. Saying straight out in front of me that the lions are his biggest attraction. That's ridiculous! *I* am. People pay to see me and my bicycles—not those animals of his."

"Yes'm," said Beeler, although she was thinking along other lines. For a fact, Miss Melinda wouldn't keep the Apaches away, not even if she was driving her chariot. Mr. Clayton was probably right. It took lions to do that.

Suddenly Miss Melinda said, "Men simply don't have tender feelings like us, dear. I'm so glad you came along today. I haven't talked to another female in ages—just to unfeeling brutes and bullies of men."

"You're right," said Beeler. "Menfolks surely don't take things to heart the way we do!" Before they found Sundown, Beeler was afraid she'd have to scratch up Leo's wishbone for some nasty remark, though she was sure he wouldn't desert her anymore. And maybe there'd have to be some knuckle scratching, too, with that scrub, Graber—even if he was bigger and older. "Miss Melinda, you know, I think I might have to beat up on both of them two I'm travelin' with before we get where we're going. I'm watchin' both of 'em good."

The bicyclienne took a lilac-smelling handkerchief out of her bosom, wiped her eyes on it, and very gently blew her nose, all the time nodding, agreeing with Beeler.

6 UNEXPECTED AUDIENCE

Three men in red flannel shirts, Clayton's helpers, came along soon to take down the tents. Miss Melinda had put on her lavender costume and a long black cloak over it. She got into her chariot and led the way to Ramada. Behind her came the camels, then a flat wagon with the two lion cages on it, driven by Mr. Clayton, and behind them the supply wagons. Leo, Nate, and Beeler with Travis brought up the rear.

That night in the adobe town of Ramada the Quineys and Nate saw their first circus. It made them gasp with wonder, just as the Spanish-talking town-folks gasped too. The performances weren't held in a tent but in a big circular corral next to a livery stable. Clayton's helpers had cleaned the corral ahead of time.

Two helpers put on white knee breeches and came out first, acting like harlequins, juggling some wooden balls in the air. After that the camels were led around the circle grunting, kneeling, and getting up again. Beeler could see that they hated bestirring themselves.

Miss Melinda came after the camels. Beeler thought she really was marvelous. She had stored her chariot and horses in the livery stable and didn't bring them out into the corral. Instead she shot out smiling on a tall, high-speed bicycle. Around and around she went, zooming until it made Beeler's head spin to watch her. It wasn't until she stopped to bow that Beeler could see the diamond-studded gold medal around her neck. The San Francisco and Oakland Bicycle Club had given it to her just the year before.

While the people of Ramada clapped, a helper brought out a very funny-looking bicycle with one great big wheel and a little bitty one. Miss Melinda rode that around too for a while. And when that was over the helper brought Blossom out on a leash and with a red collar around her neck. Under his arm he carried one wheel only.

Everybody gasped some more. Blossom wasn't yawning now but showing her fangs. Dauntless Daniel didn't do a single thing to tame her down. He stood watching from the door of the livery stable while Miss Melinda blew kisses to the audience. Then she got up on the one wheel, still smiling, balanced there for a time, and took the leash from the helper. With Blossom traveling by her side, the bicyclienne went slowly around the corral in the opposite direction from the one she had taken on the other wheels. Then she reversed. As she went faster and faster, the lioness trotted or cantered or galloped. And then it was all over. Miss Melinda got off and curtseyed while the people clapped. Blossom let out a cough, then yawned.

Next it was Mr. Clayton's turn. He had barrels for Charlie to jump on to and off of when he yelled "Up" and "Down" at the lion. Charlie snarled and clawed the air a couple of times, but that was all he did except for jumping and swishing his tail when Clayton cracked his whip.

Finally came the pretty-baby contest. It cost the folks of Ramada ten cents to vote once for the handsomest baby in town. Miss Melinda held up each contest baby and walked around the corral with it. Then a helper collected the ten-cent pieces. The prettiest baby raked in ninety cents for the circus—most of which, Beeler noticed, came from the baby's pa. For a prize the bicyclienne kissed the baby on the forehead. It bawled.

The circus was over. The helpers walked around with hats in their hands, collecting whatever folks would throw in. Because it seemed the polite thing to do and she was traveling with the circus, Beeler took off her hat and collected, too. She got one American silver dollar, a Mexican peso, two other Mexican coins she couldn't recognize, a silver button, and a piece of blue-green rock that might be turquoise. She decided Mexicans were generous folks and said *"Gracias"* a lot, a Spanish word she already knew. Nobody here seemed to care she came from Texas. But maybe they didn't know. She didn't tell anyone either.

Miss Melinda was tickled when Beeler gave her what was in her hat. She took the button and the rock and gave the rest to Mr. Clayton, who was sort of pleased too. "We've made enough to get to Silverado," Beeler heard him tell his bicyclienne. "We'll buy some supplies here, and tomorrow morning we'll start on our way."

There were lanterns set on the ground behind the corral railings. Their light blocked out what was beyond them. Beeler knew, though, what was west of Ramada—mountains, great big ones. She hoped Miss Melinda didn't plan to travel through them in her chariot. Horses and four-wheel wagons would probably have a hard enough time. Going up and down steep Ramada Hill had taught her that lesson.

For a fact, they *were* traveling with the circus! Nate, speaking Spanish, had asked everybody he'd met in Ramada if they'd ever heard of Sunset, Sundown, or Puesta del Sol? Nobody had.

The bicyclienne drove a wagon with Nate riding beside her. Packed inside it was her chariot, filled with bicycles. Beeler on Jinglebob, with Travis alongside, rode next to the wagon. Leo rode with one of Clayton's handlers, the man who looked after the camels. Two Cents and Stupid were tied to the back of the bicycle wagon because they just refused to be anywhere near the lions or camels. Mr. Clayton decided they annoyed the animals, too, so he kept them out of the way. Jinglebob, though, got along just fine with everybody, especially Miss Melinda, who fussed over him. One thing was true about him, Beeler had to admit. He surely appreciated being admired. He was like two-legged folks that way.

The mountains weren't much like the stereopticon slides Beeler had seen once you were into them. They weren't snowy, probably because it was July and hot by now. At least it was hot during the daytime, hot enough to ride in shirtsleeves. As they went up a narrow path into the pine-covered mountains, Beeler did some deep pondering about Miss Melinda and Mr. Clayton. It seemed to her that the bicyclienne had given up a lot to be part of his circus. She'd said she could work in any circus in the whole world! To think he liked lions better than he liked her. Where were his tender feelings?

Sometimes Beeler glanced at Graber up on the wagon seat out of the corner of one eye. For a while she'd suspected he might have some tender feelings somewhere, but after what he'd done in Deadahead, she doubted it. It appeared to her that sometimes she positively seemed to be bothersome to him. Or at least he acted that way.

The mountains were plumb full of deer. One of Clayton's helpers was a good rifle shot, so there was always venison when they stopped at night. They went through canyons and along ridges by day, but at dusk Clayton called a halt in some flat place beside a stream. This was so the horses and Travis could graze. The lions tolerated venison just fine.

Beeler was happy to share Miss Melinda's nice tent and sleep on her rug, because it got breezy and cold at night up so high. To enjoy the rug she had to drink sassafras tea, though, with the bicyclienne to thin their blood for summer. But she said no to drinking the canteen water Miss Melinda had dropped a rusty nail into to put iron into a person. It tasted like water a rusty nail had been dropped into.

Leo and Nate slept under the wagons with the helpers, out of the wind, while the lions in their cages went into Clayton's tent so they wouldn't catch cold.

Beeler talked to Nate and Leo about Mr. Clayton and the lions the third night in the mountains. This time they camped in a little meadow ringed around by big rocks. The Texans were squatting by a fire of their own, drinking coffee when Beeler spoke up. "Miss Melinda says she thinks Blossom and Charlie sleep on

Dauntless Daniel's bed with him. He lets them out of their cages."

Leo shook his head, swallowed a mouthful of beans, and said, "No, I got curious and peeked under his tent. I seen his bed. It ain't that big. Blossom was the only lion laying on his bed. That's because she's the littlest. Charlie, he sleeps beside the bed. He's sort of a carpet for Mr. Clayton's bare feet."

Beeler exploded, "Holy snakes, are they that tame?"

Leo nodded. "Mr. Clayton, he told me once that he brought 'em up from kittens, both of 'em. The only reason he keeps 'em in cages is because otherwise they might run off and try to join up with some mountain panthers and get clawed up bad or killed."

Nate took a swallow of coffee. "That probably explains why they're yawning all the time. They must be bored."

Beeler asked Leo, "Why does Charlie let out those growlin' sounds when Mr. Clayton makes him jump up on barrels?"

"Clayton says it's because Charlie just hates to work. Blossom hates to work, too. That's why she shows her teeth when the chariot lady drags her around on a rope."

Beeler was stunned at all Leo knew. "Is it because he worries so much about his lions that Mr. Clayton's goin' gray-headed?"

Leo shook his head. "Nope, he told me about that,

too. It's because of all them women who've tried to catch him over the years. He says womenfolks fuss over him somethin' terrible. That's the way they act around lion tamers. They want to tame the tamers. He's inclined to be bilious, particularly when he loses at poker. That's really what's wrong between him and the chariot lady."

"What?" Beeler wanted to know.

"He thinks she's purty, but she keeps after him to take Morley's Vitalizer and use goose-grease gizzard oil on his chest when he gets a cold—not to mention rust water and sassafras tea."

Beeler nodded. "I know all about them last two. I drew the line at rust water myself. Miss Melinda's mighty set in her ways when it comes to fussin' over folks."

"Rust water would make a bobcat bilious," said Leo disgustedly as he stood up.

Beeler knew that Leo didn't take much to circus life. Looking after camels was lots worse than taking care of horses. He'd already complained that camels could spit in your face. One had got him right between the eyes, and he'd taken it hard.

"I'll take a good look at Travis and Jinglebob while I'm lookin' at Two Cents," he told his sister. "It's awful quiet out there tonight."

"Aw right," she warned, "take a look, but keep out

of my critter's horn range. You know he don't favor ya, Leo."

She turned to Nate after Leo had left. "I don't know why he felt called on to do that, Graber. Nights have been quiet all along up here, haven't you noticed?"

"Yes, Beulah Land, I have. That's because of the lions and probably the camels too. Wild animals don't like anything strange around. And you have to admit— Blossom and Charlie are strange!"

"That's prob'ly so." She changed the subject. "Miss Melinda's sufferin' from unrequited love. Would you know anythin' about that?"

"Maybe."

Beeler waited for him to go on while she watched Miss Melinda at the other fire, stirring venison stew in a big cook pot. She didn't keep her eyes on Nate's face because that wouldn't have been very polite, but she'd had one glimpse that had told her he knew something about unrequited love all right.

But he never got to explain about it because Leo came back too soon. He wasn't running. As a matter of fact, he wasn't even walking fast. But there was something about the way he was moving that made both Beeler and Nate look up at him. Leo was whiter in the face than a wash boiled for three days on the back of a hot stove. He spoke before they could ask what ailed him. "There are Indians out in the rocks.

Some of 'em are sittin' on top of the rocks watchin' us. I seen 'em good. Some got white paint on their chests."

Nate reached up and grabbed Leo's arm and pulled him down to kneel beside the fire. "Beulah Land, pour Leo some more coffee. You two sit here and drink it while I go tell Mr. Clayton."

Her hands trembling as badly as Leo's, Beeler poured coffee. Some of it got into her brother's cup. As Nate walked off to the other campfire, she asked softly, "Leo, are you dead sure you ain't seein' things that ain't there?"

"No, they're on the rocks. I figure they're all around us. Apaches for sure. What d'ya know about Apaches?"

"Nothin', except what you heard too. They favor mule and horsemeat. Nate knows somethin' about Comanches. I sure hope he knows what he's doin' now. Apaches ain't Comanches, and one kinda Indian's diff'runt from another kinda Indian. That's somethin' a lot a folks don't know. They think all Indians is the same." Beeler knew she was chattering to keep her courage up. She went right on babbling like a lost turkey until Nate came back.

He didn't say a word to her and Leo. Instead, he got up, just as white as Leo had been, on top of a tree stump, waved his arms in the air and did a queer sort of stomping dance. Then he started to yell—not in English but in Spanish.

Leo whispered to his sister, "He's gone loco. Scared plumb outa his mind. The Apaches'll put a arrow into him." Leo got up, but Beeler hauled him down again.

From flat on the ground, she saw how the circus folks were moving around. They'd heard what Nate had said to the lion tamer. The helpers weren't running—even if they were moving very fast. One was taking Charlie's barrels out of a wagon. Another was dragging the bicycles down. Miss Melinda had trotted into her tent right away.

The third handler came up onto the stump the minute Nate got off it. He'd brought three wooden balls with him and began to juggle them. Nate yelled some more, standing beside him.

And now something happened. Long-haired men with red-flannel bands around their foreheads and high leather moccasins came out to the edge of the wagons. Some of them did have white paint on their bare chests. The rest had what looked like long night-shirts down to the calves of their legs. They had paint on their faces. Three of them had Winchesters, the others, all nine of them, had bows. There wasn't a feather on any one of them.

While the juggler went on, the other handlers set up Charlie's barrels. Clayton let the lion out of his cage the second the juggler had finished and shouted at him to get "Up." Charlie growled but jumped up onto the smallest barrel.

Beeler saw that the Apaches didn't move back one bit when Charlie came out, but they watched every move he made as he went through his downs and ups on the barrels.

When Clayton was through, he called out, "Melinda." She didn't come, though. Beeler guessed why. That costume took so long to get into with all those little bitty hooks and eyes. If a person was nervous, it'd take even longer.

Beeler found the courage to get up to sit beside Leo. She poked him with her finger. "Leo, you get up and do somethin' to keep the Apaches lookin'."

He squeaked at her, "Holy gatlins, what'll I do?"

"Walk on your hands. The way you do at home. Stand on your head. Do anythin', but do it now. Miss Melinda's bogged down in somethin'."

Leo got to his feet shaking all over. But he flung up his hands and did a wobbly cartwheel. Then three more. Finally he stood on his head, waving his legs in the air, and then for a couple of yards walked on his hands. Finally he collapsed, panting, a foot or two from Beeler. The Apaches had watched every single thing he did without moving.

Beeler took a breath all the way down to her boots. It was up to her now. She got up and started to sing.

The first thing that came to her mind was "Nearer My God to Thee."

Nate knew that hymn tune, too. He came beside her to sing it through. And when they were finished, he started in on "Evalina." He put his arms around Beeler's waist and waltzed her around the campfires while the Indians went on looking. When they were through "Evalina" and were about to start the third time on it, which was very hard work in that altitude, Miss Melinda finally showed up.

She came out this time in black and blue spangles and dark-blue tights. She grabbed the bicycle nearest her tent, which turned out to be the unicycle. And once she was on it she started cycling so fast that Clayton couldn't hand Blossom to her, though he ran after her with the lionness on her leash.

Marvelous Melinda was doing the act all alone, meandering in and out in the places that weren't too bumpy. And she was smiling and waving at the Indians. The light from the two campfires made the one turning wheel twinkle red and her dark spangles glow like coals of scarlet fire. When she'd finished, Melinda poised on her unicycle for a minute, blowing kisses to the Apaches just as she had to the people of Ramada.

The Indians didn't clap, but they didn't go away either. They just stood staring. Finally one of the Apaches carrying a Winchester stepped out ahead of the others. Beeler's hand went to her waistline under her jacket. Leo's Winchester was by the fire along with Nate's. They hadn't dared to pick up their guns.

The Indian came straight toward the bicyclienne. She'd got off her unicycle and was standing beside it, holding it up. The Apache walked slowly, but Mr. Clayton moved fast. He ran out and planted himself in front of the lady. "Boy," he called out to Nate. "Tell this Indian he can have anything in this circus except for Miss Holcomb!"

Nate spoke in Spanish to the Apache, who only gazed at him. The Indian kept right on walking, but as he did he put out one hand and gave Clayton a shove out of the way. While Nate went on in Spanish, the Apache circled the bicyclienne, who had a frozen smile on her face. Then all of a sudden he reached out and grabbed the shining unicycle from her. He tucked it under his arm, turned his back on Clayton and Miss Melinda, and walked back to the other Apaches. They moved aside to let him through and, when he was gone, turned around and followed him.

"Ah-h-h!" cried the bicyclienne, flinging herself into the lion tamer's arms.

"My Melinda!" came from him.

Beeler sank down onto her heels. She felt weak as mush in the knees. Leo and Graber came over now too.

Leo's face was sweating. Graber had gone greeny-pale.

"What'd you say just now to the Indians?" Beeler asked Nate.

"That the squaw was Dauntless Daniel's. I said what he wanted me to say—that they could have anything else in the circus but her."

"I don't think the Indian ever did want her," said Leo. "He wanted that wheel."

"You're right, Leo," agreed Beeler. "Apaches must have plenty of squaws of their own. But one thing they haven't got is bicycles."

"They haven't got lions either," came from Leo. "I woulda took a lion."

Beeler glanced at Miss Melinda, who was bawling on the lion tamer's chest, wetting him down plenty. It appeared to her that Mr. Clayton and the bicyclienne had come to a meeting of minds. Clayton looked like he was taking to her like honeysuckle to a front porch.

Beeler let out a sigh while she looked at Nate. He'd surely used his head back there when the Apaches showed up out of nowhere. If he hadn't, they might all be dead by now or all their horses taken away. What if he'd picked up his Winchester and started shooting out into the dark? No, he was plenty smart. She thought back to their talk about unrequited love and wondered what he'd meant by that one word—"maybe."

She wondered, too, the rest of the next day while

she led Jinglebob down a steep place how an Apache
Indian would let folks know he'd like a performance.
She wasn't so scared now that she could think some
about it and see the odd side of giving a show for
Indians.

Leo, up ahead of her on the trail, must have been
pondering the same thing. He called back, "If you and
me had passed the hat to the Indians, what dya suppose
we'd of got?"

"A arrow in our gizzards, more'n likely." Then she
said, "You done real fine back there. You walked good
on your hands."

She heard him laughing. "By gatlins, you said somethin' nice to me, Beeler."

"Hang on to it, Leo. It might be the last time before
we find Sundown."

There was a Mexican town just out of the mountains, but Mr. Clayton and Miss Melinda didn't get
married there. The bicyclienne told Beeler that she
wanted to be able to understand the preacher's words.
Beeler understood. She wasn't sure she'd trust Clayton that much either—or any other man. She thought
it would be smart to wait until they got to Silverado,
too, and found a sin buster who talked English.

The country west of the mountains was a high plain,
swept over by winds all the time. It was hot, and so was

the dust that blew into their faces. All of the circus
people and the Texans wore handkerchiefs over their
noses and mouths, but the poor animals couldn't.
Jinglebob and Travis snorted a lot, and the lions
coughed even more. Mr. Clayton kept the circus away
from the dangerous White Sands. It gave Beeler the
willies just hearing about them. Even the bugs were
white out there, Clayton said. West of the sands was
another Mexican town where they gave a show in front
of the one hotel. That show gave them more money to
get to Silverado, where they expected to do right well.

It was yucca country from now on—high desert that
had waves in it. Beeler wasn't so interested in the tall
plants as she was in the deserted adobe houses that had
once been way stations for the old Butterfield Stage
Line. They made fine camping places for the circus.
She had got over her wariness of mountains, and it was
a good thing too. Just about everywhere she looked,
there they were—purple in the distance. New Mexico
Territory wasn't like any parts of Texas she'd ever set
eyes on. They were carrying water and hay for the
horses and camels now. As Clayton said, the country
ought to be camel country, but not even camels did
well in it. Travis kept swinging his head from side to
side and planting his hooves in the sandy dirt, pawing
until Beeler whistled him on. He didn't think this was
like Texas either.

Before they got to Silverado the circus went through another little Mexican town that had copper mines all around it. Nate had told the Quineys that mines were deep holes with underground tunnels going off them. At least silver mines were like that and gold mines, too. But copper mines were holes right on top of the ground. According to the Mexicans nearby, these were old, old mines. Indian prisoners of the Spanish conquerors of Mexico had dug copper in them a long, long time ago. Beeler thought that was mighty interesting information. A person learned things traveling.

Silverado was different too. It took a bit of a climb to get there, but it was worth it. It was nearly two miles up in the sky. Because there were trees in the mountains not too far away, Silverado's houses were made out of wood. There were a lot of saloons, of course, and a couple of hotels and stores. But there was something else: gold and silver bricks lying on the boardwalk outside the offices of shipping companies.. Everybody in the circus had his eyes sticking out so far you could have knocked them off with a board as they rode by the piles of yellow and white bricks. The ore had been melted down in Silvarado's smelters and shaped into bricks to be carried to San Francisco. Nobody laid a hand on the bricks, not even the drivers of the fourteen-horse teams that went up and down the street all day and all night, going to and coming from mines around Silverado. Beeler longed to heft a brick of gold just to see how heavy it was but decided not to.

Mr. Clayton and Miss Melinda found a preacher in Silverado, and he married them in the parlor of the best hotel in town. A circus helper stood up with the lion tamer. The hotel owner's little bitty wife stood up with the bicyclienne, who had on her purple outfit. Even though she'd never set eyes on Marvelous Melinda before, the hotel lady bawled. Beeler didn't understand why. Getting double harnessed wasn't that bad. Lots of folks got married and lived to a ripe old age.

Afterwards Beeler said to Leo, "I heard every word the preacher said. She roped, throwed, and branded him just fine. Very legallike." She eyed Graber, who was looking out the hotel window past the bride and groom. He and Leo had been moseying around Silverado earlier that day while she'd talked a livery stable man into seeing to it that Jinglebob and Travis got a special feed. It had cost her twenty-five cents to get it done, but the critters were resting easy, side by side, though not in the same stall. The man hadn't cottoned to the thought that longhorns belonged in stables, but he looked at it differently when Beeler told him, using Nate's expression, that the steer was a child's pet. Graber had been pretty smart to say that. Using it worked just fine.

Nate finally turned his head to look at her. He grinned. "A man in the Silverado Emporium told me just before the ceremony that he's heard there's a town called Sunrise Flats or something like that in Arizona Territory."

"Has he been there?" Beeler wanted to know.

"No, but he says a miner coming east talked about it. We'll start for there in the morning. I told Mr. Clayton just before he got married that we were leaving."

Leo asked, "Did you hear about your pa and them four other galoots?"

"No, they don't seem to have been here, but that doesn't prove much. Silverado's a busy place. Nobody knew Mr. McCarty's brother here either."

Beeler laughed. "That ain't no cause to wonder. I bet he's dropped his name in the river and is usin' a new one now."

"I don't know," came from Graber. "The man who told me about Sunrise Flats said Silverado has lots of hangings but no robberies to speak of. I almost hate to leave it. He said, 'Nowhere on God's footstool are women and children safer!' "

Beeler had to smile. She reckoned she knew why. In Silverado a person got hanged before he did anything that was against the law. That's why gold and silver were out on the walks in plain sight.

"Is Arizona Territory like this here one?" Leo asked.

"Are they sort of against us Texans there, too?"

Beeler listened closely. She guessed they'd been lucky so far. Nobody had made anything of their being from Texas.

Nate said, "I don't know how they feel about Texans there, Leo. The man said Arizona Territory was maybe a bit wilder even than it is hereabouts. It's lots hotter—lower down and more lonesome."

Beeler pondered this without joy. Finally she said, "That's what the preacher back home in Cottonwood used to say about hell!"

Nate agreed. "That crossed my mind, too, Beulah Land."

7 "HIS TOWN"

Miss Melinda, or really Mrs. Duckworth or Mrs. Clayton, gave Leo and Nate each a kiss on the cheek the next morning but dragged Beeler aside before the Texans rode out of Silverado. She took a piece of black ribbon out of her reticule. Two little five-dollar gold pieces with holes in them hung from the ribbon, which she tied around Beeler's neck under her shirt collar.

"Holy snakes, I didn't earn these and my neck's not clean, ma'am."

"I know," said the bicyclienne, "but I want you to have them. Mr. Clayton likes my gold and diamond medal, but he doesn't like to see my presents from old beaux. He thought you and the boys did just wonderfully when the Apaches came. He's too shy to tell you. But you were real performers! You went right along with his idea to give a benefit performance for the Indians." She smiled. "My dear, before you go, I want you to buy something for me at the store." Now she gave Beeler a silver dollar, too.

"What do you want?"

"A large bottle of liver regulator and a little one of Thompsan's Hair Dye, brown in color. And a bar of Pears soap for you. The regulator and hair dye are for Mr. Clayton."

Beeler nodded. She'd forget to buy the soap. "Anythin' you want for the lions?"

"No, I'll try to stop their coughing later." She laughed. "Do you suppose a lion has ever had lard and turpentine rubbed onto its chest? It's a wonderful remedy for coughs."

"No, ma'am." Beeler thought with pity of poor Blossom and Charlie. It was her horseback opinion that the lions would get washed pretty soon. Mrs. Clayton was soap-and-water crazy. She'd never believe it was natural for lions to cough. That's what Dauntless Daniel had told Nate once.

It was high time to skedaddle from the circus!

One of the gold pieces bought supplies for the Texans to take them to Sunrise Flats. The other one they'd keep dangling around Beeler's neck until they needed it. And Nate still had some jingle in his pockets. If they found his pa in Sunrise Flats, Nate said, they wouldn't need money. Mr. Graber would take care of all of them and be happy to pay travelers bound east for Texas to let the two Quineys travel home with them.

Beeler didn't say anything to Nate about her suspicions, but the morning they rode out of Silverado she dropped back to ride beside Leo for a while. It took some hard jerking on Travis's neck rope to make him behave because he hadn't taken to livery-stable life one bit, and he wanted to run loose.

"Leo," she said, "my cow sense tells me that we hadn't better count too much on Graber's pa doin' anythin' for us except mebbe sayin' 'thank you kindly.' Him and those men with him! Don't it seem queer to you that nobody we talked to has ever set eyes on 'em except that woman in Lovelock and then old Billy-whiskers and that wife of his who fed you cake in Deadahead. No one else seein' hide or hair of 'em means somethin' to me if it don't to you."

"What?" Leo was being scornful again.

"They don't want to be seen. They're keepin' away from towns and tradin' posts. There's only one reason why they'd do that. They're up to devilment."

He scoffed, "Nate's pa used to be a wisdom bringer, remember? Do you think a teacher'd be up to devilment?"

Beeler nodded her head and looked wise. "If they set their minds to it, they could do it better'n most folks could, I bet. They're plenty smart. And, too, they can get ideas out of books that are wicked. I heard tell there are lots of wicked books."

Leo hooted. "Next thing you'll be sayin' is that preachers can hatch up devilment, too."

Again Beeler nodded. "A sin buster who goes bad—he's the worst kind of all. Nerissa claimed she knew one once who ran away with the Christmas collection plate and the only singer in the choir who could carry a tune in a 'tater sack. Everybody missed the singer real bad."

Satisfied with the expression of shock on her brother's face, she whistled to Travis and went up to ride behind Nate. Her eyes on his widish back, she murmured to herself, "Poor cuss. Down in my gizzard I have the feelin' he mebbe ain't gonna have much good news comin' whenever he does find this here Sundown. But I'm gonna try to make it up to him. After all there's only one of him and eleven of us Quineys left as far as I know. If he hitches up someday with me, that'd make him half a Quiney and never lonesome again."

She glanced around her as they left Silverado. That town had smelled pleasantly of fresh-cut lumber. It had been interesting, too, with all the gold and silver lying around loose. She liked traveling, even with Leo along to cramp her a bit. She thought pityingly of

Nerissa and the other Texas womenfolks she knew. They were surely bogged down in carpets. All the traveling most of the women in Cottonwood did was walking around their coffeepot on the stove looking for the handle!

The road to Sunrise Flats led southwest, according to Nate. It was only a trail that wandered between more mountains, mostly through forests. The country was plenty wild. Beeler knew it was grizzly bear territory, though they never saw one the nights they camped. But they heard catamounts wailing in the timber and coyotes too. Leo shot a buck deer that ran over the trail in front of them, so they saved on supplies. The venison lasted them two days. Although Apaches were supposed to live in this part of New Mexico Territory too, they didn't catch sight of one Indian. Anyway folks in Silverado had said that they weren't the same kind of Apaches as around Ramada. Maybe these Indians didn't take any interest in three folks traveling together, or they were too poor looking to bother with.

Travis looked to be thinning down some more now that the grazing hadn't been so fine. He couldn't hang behind here and graze because once you rode beyond a bend in the trail you lost sight of anything behind you. He hated pine cones. Beeler wouldn't lose him to Indians or catamounts or grizzlies. Sometimes she felt guilty over him. Poor little critter. She hadn't planned to fetch him so far from Santa Rosa County. What he was doing now wasn't natural for a steer. But Travis had surely earned his keep. There wasn't a finer watch animal anywhere, even if he hadn't given warning about the Indians. What was more, Beeler suspected just seeing Travis, who looked a lot fiercer than he was, kept wild things, four-legged and two-legged, away.

Sunrise Flats, the Texans discovered when they got there, was where the man in Silverado had said it would be. But that wasn't what folks who lived there called it now. The Quineys and Nate learned the new name five minutes after they rode into town. That was because of Travis and because of the town dogs. There must have been twenty of them, Beeler decided later, though in the uproar she didn't have time to make a head count.

The minute the Texans passed the blacksmith's shop at the very end of town, the dogs showed up. They came pouring out of an alley between the blacksmith's and a saloon like dried peas from a split sack, all of them yapping and barking.

Nate shouted over them, "Hark, hark the dogs do bark!" He could do that because Stupid stood quiet and let them snap at him. Two Cents reared, while

Jinglebob let fly with his hooves at a couple of dogs before Beeler pulled up on his reins. Travis was the real troublemaker. Because he hated dogs he let out a bellow and jerked on his neck rope, pulling the saddle horn he'd been tied to clear off. Then he was gone, charging down the street.

Yelling and whistling, Beeler galloped after him. The dogs deserted Stupid and Two Cents and came dashing at Jinglebob's heels. Everybody in town stopped what he was doing to watch as the black steer went rumbling past, bellowing, hooking his head to the left and then to the right. Ladies with market baskets on their arms quivered behind porch posts. People came out of stores to stand on the boardwalk, then leap back as Travis hooked toward them. Windows were opened and heads poked out while Beeler went on whistling, scared that somebody would shoot Travis.

A little Mexican boy in a big straw hat stood in front of one saloon. He yelled out, *"Toro, toro."* He was laughing until Travis all at once switched direction and headed straight for him with the dogs at his heels. The boy lunged to one side only a second before Travis lumbered through the saloon's swinging doors. All the dogs ran under them after him.

Beeler drew Jinglebob up and listened. Lordy, what a hollering and yelling and uproar of barks and bellows! Glass was being broken everywhere, she reckoned, judging from the tinkly crashing sounds. She looked over her shoulder. There wasn't going to be any help from Nate or Leo. No such luck! Nate couldn't get Stupid started on his way, and Two Cents was still pawing the sky with his front hooves. Beeler dropped the reins over Jinglebob's head to make him stay and slid off. She looked at the saloon and shook her head. But she went up its steps anyway. Beeler knew all about saloons. Nerissa always made her and the weaner gals cross the street from Cottonwood's saloons, they were so wicked. It made walking down the street a bunch of zigs and zags because there were so many places of sin. And it made the Quineys, all of them, keep quiet about the bottle of whiskey Nerissa's husband kept out in the barn under the hay.

Saloons were the hatching places of devilment. Wary of what devilment she might be getting into, Beeler went through the double doors, too—but nowhere near as fast as Travis and the dogs had.

What a sight she saw! Travis in the middle of the floor with broken tables and chairs all around him. Spilled beer and whiskey made wet spots all over the sawdust. A whole ring of dogs surrounded Travis, snarling and barking. Now and then he'd rush one, and it would move back. A whole ring of people surrounded the dogs. Some of them were up against the walls, others in corners barricaded behind chairs and

hat racks. Three ladies in short dresses were up on the
long wooden bar that ran from one end of the saloon
to the other. One of them let out a screech when she
caught sight of Beeler.

Beeler called to her, "Don't yell so. The critter belongs to me. I've come to save him." She walked toward the circle of dogs. They were just common ordinary pot hounds as far as she could see. "You get outa
my way," she told two of them, lifting her boot. They
moved aside, snarling, so she could get to Travis, who
was trembling. She spoke loudly to him, so everybody
would know he was hers. "They ain't nothin' to be
scared of—jest old flea-trap dogs." She took him by
one horn and by the neck rope. Then she told the
saloon folks, "I got my critter. Now you get your dogs
away from him."

A big man wearing a white apron, which was an odd
thing on a man, came from behind the bar where the
ladies were standing. He had two brooms in his hands.
He gave one to another man and together they began
to sweep the dogs out onto the street. Most of them
went willingly enough, although a couple yelped on
the way. Leo and Nate came in during the second wave
of dogs going out.

The white-aproned man had a mouth alive with
gold teeth. He asked Beeler when the dogs were all

gone, "Who's gonna pay for my busted furniture and glasses? And all that spilled liquor?"

Beeler, who was patting Travis to keep him calmed down, asked in turn, "Ask them dogs to pay ya, Mister. They started it the minute we set hoof in this town of yours. What kinda welcome do you folks in Sunrise Flats give strangers anyhow?"

"Texans, ain't ya?" asked the man.

"We're only passing through," Nate added hastily.

While people came away from the walls, and the ladies were helped down off the bar, Nate explained his errand. The saloon man shook his head. "This town used to be Sunrise Flats, but it ain't anymore. I never heard tell of Sunset or Sundown. I never seen five men like you describe 'em. Maybe they went somewheres else in this town and then rode on west."

Beeler noticed that Nate's tale had seemed to soften Mr. Goldtooth the way it seemed to soften other folks. It made them feel sorry. She decided it was time to make tracks out of the saloon with her critter before the man asked again who'd pay for the damage to the busted things. The stink of the liquor wasn't one bit pleasant either.

She'd started to lead Travis out when all at once the man asked, "Who'd you three boys be?"

Nate was gallant, even if he put her last in line.

"This is Leo Quiney and I'm Jonathan Graber. That's Beulah Land Quiney with the steer."

Beeler lifted her hat. "I'm a she, not a he. The critter ain't theirs. He belongs to me. He's named Travis. He's never been in a saloon before."

"*Travis?*" The saloon man looked as if somebody had just hit him over the head with a club.

"Did you say *Travis?*" one of the saloon ladies asked.

"That's what we call him."

Everybody started to laugh. While Beeler and the boys looked on puzzled, all the folks in the saloon bent double, laughing. When the saloon man quit leaning against the bar to support himself and wiped his eyes with his apron, he said, "Forget about the damage your steer's caused, girlie. It was worth it, every busted chair and table and glass."

Now it was really time to get out of there, away from all these lunatics. "Much obliged," said Beeler, as she hauled Travis out of the Gay Lady Saloon, over its porch, and down into the dusty street of the town. Whatever the town was named now, it surely wasn't much to look at. It was on a flat piece of ground with some big rocky hills not far off, so she could see why it had been called Flats once. The town was made of adobe houses and false-fronted wooden stores and saloons. As she and the boys stood in the street, Beeler noticed the red brick building across from them. The

gold-painted sign on its windows read *Travis Bank*.
She looked to its left. There was a store there. Its
black-and-white painted sign was *Travis General Emporium*. Two doors away she spotted the name again:
Travis Undertaking Parlor. Now she turned to look
behind her, and in a row she spied: *Travis Sundries
and Medicines, Travis Saddlery,* and *Travis Hand
Laundry.*

"I guess this town has to be named Travis?" she
said to Nate, who had also been looking around.

"I guess so." He seemed down at the mouth. "Leo
and I'll tackle some of the other saloons and ask
about my father and Sundown or Sunset. As long as
we're here, I suppose we ought to find out everything
we can. Please stay with the horses and your animal."

"You think I shouldn't go inside saloons?" Beeler
was touched at Nate's thoughtfulness. She was smiling
as she watched him and Leo head into the saloon next
door to the Gay Lady. She kept right on smiling as
she watched the boys walk back and forth across the
street from one den of devilment to another. There
wasn't a dog in sight. Travis was king of the street.

"You done just fine in there," she told him. "You
done better bustin' up a saloon than the temperance
ladies in Cottonwood coulda in the same amount of
time." Destroying the town saloons was one of Nerissa's dreams.

Suddenly Travis jerked his head, alerting Beeler. Somebody was coming out of an alley toward them. Whoever it was appeared odd because it wore black floppy pants, a black jacket, and a little round black hat. The person had black hair in one long braid down its back and sort of yellow skin. When whoever it was got within spitting distance, Beeler saw a mustache. It wasn't a lady then, but what else it was she surely didn't know.

The man in black smiled. "Little Master, Big Missy sent me to see you."

Beeler had caught the words "Little Master." She let out a sigh and took off her hat. "I ain't your master, Mister. I'm a she. Who'd you be? Don't come too close to my critter's horns!"

"I Po Wing. Very fine animal with horns, Little Missy's. Big Missy want me ask you come to her house now."

"What's a Po Wing?"

"Me. Chinese man."

"Ah." Now Beeler understood. She'd never laid eyes on anyone from China. But the schoolmarm in Cottonwood had told them about China, over the ocean from California.

Po Wing said again, "You please to come to Big Missy's house."

"Who's Big Missy?"

"Boss lady. Missus Travis. Missus Louie Travis. She very big boss."

"What does she want me for?"

Po Wing stuck out a finger at Travis. "She want to talk about that animal. Boss lady hear that he come to town. I think Big Missy want to give you money for him."

Beeler drew back. For sure, it hadn't been cow country they'd just traveled through, though there'd been some sheep about. Did Mrs. Travis hanker for beef? "I ain't sellin' him, Mr. Po Wing."

Po Wing shook his head. "Boss lady don't want to buy him. She want *see* him and you. She say come now."

Beeler looked around her. There were quite a few people standing on the walks in front of stores. All of them were staring at her and Travis; quite a few of them were grinning. Neither Nate nor Leo was in sight.

Making up her mind because of the mention of money, Beeler hitched Jinglebob to the same rail with Two Cents and Stupid. She'd take Travis with her if that's what Mrs. Travis wanted. "Hey, Mister," Beeler called out to a man sitting on a chair outside the funeral parlor. "Will you tell them boys I'm ridin' with that I went to Mrs. Travis's house with Mr. Po Wing? Do you know him or where the house would be?" Beeler came closer. Would the Chinese want to rob her of the gold piece around her neck? "Mister," she asked softly, "can I trust Mr. Po Wing?"

"You surely can. He's the most honest man in town. As for the house, it's the only brick place except for Mr. Travis's bank building. I'll send the boys there if you ain't back soon. Good luck to ya."

"I'd be obliged to ya." Beeler took the steer's neck rope, told him, "Come along, Travis. Somebody else's prob'ly got it in mind to admire you," and followed Po Wing down the middle of the street.

Boss Lady's house was yellow brick, not red, and it was good sized. It looked more like a courthouse than a place to sleep and eat in. Beeler wondered about the inside of it, but she never got to see it.

Mrs. Travis came outside, slamming the front door behind her, before Beeler, the steer, and Po Wing were even there. She was a sight! She had frizzled red-brown hair, a set of bottom teeth that rose up out of her lower jaw when she tried to look pleasant, and a scrooched-up expression. She looked a lot like one of the flea-trap dogs in town. But what was more she was beef to the hocks—surely a solid woman. Because the sun was out and hot, Mrs. Travis had a parasol up over her head. It was ruffled and pale pink to match her dress. They suited her the way a sidesaddle suited a hog.

"I am Missus Travis, Mrs. Mimi Travis," she said in a highfalutin voice.

Because she was talking woman to woman, Beeler lifted her hat. "Yes, ma'am," she told her.

Mrs. Travis put her handkerchief to her nose. Through it she wanted to know, "What is that black beast with you called?"

"Travis, ma'am. We're from Texas."

"I am told he caused consternation in a saloon here in my husband's absence on business in San Francisco. Your animal is obstreperous."

Beeler didn't know if these big words were good or bad. She said, "Dogs run him into a saloon, if that's what you got in mind. It wasn't my Travis's fault."

The woman snorted through the handkerchief. "You realize, of course, that this town is named for my husband, who founded it last year?"

Being polite, Beeler told her, "It appears to me he owns it. His brand looks to be on jest about everythin' in it. Didn't it used to be called Sunrise Flats?" Beeler saw Po Wing grinning behind the woman where she couldn't see him. Beeler guessed it was the only place he ever dared to grin.

Mrs. Travis took down the handkerchief. Her face was a pure caution. For a fact, she had a mean disposition and right now meant murder. "My husband made this town what it is. Its name has been changed to honor him. He is its most important citizen. He is the mayor. It is *his town*. He *never* goes into saloons. He must not be made a laughingstock of by a cow from Texas."

"Travis ain't a cow. Travis is a steer."

This made Mrs. Travis clap the handkerchief back real fast and talk through it some more. "Whatever he is, he smells strongly of cow. Or you do. I can't tell which. What would you ask of me to get you to leave town with him right now—this very instant?"

It was on the tip of Beeler's tongue to cuss her out, but she thought better of it. Mrs. Travis was offering cash money to get rid of Travis! Now she knew what the Chinese servant had meant about money. "Hang and rattle. Don't fight your head," she told herself, wondering how much to ask for. Then she took a deep breath and said, "Twenty dollars, and we'll light out right away. Cash on the barrelhead, too."

"Give this little road agent from Texas twenty dollars, Po Wing," snapped the woman. She handed her reticule to him, then with her hand on the front doorknob said, "Perhaps you wonder, girl, why civilized people in New Mexico and Arizona Territory don't like Texans. Half of you are desperate characters escaping justice—wanted even in Texas. The rest of you are out to make the territories part of Texas. What is your name? I have every intention of asking the sheriff about you, let me warn you!"

After the Chinese had given Beeler one double eagle and she'd pocketed it, she called out, "Bertha Mae Muller." Mrs. Travis wouldn't check out the name Quiney they'd used in the Gay Lady Saloon. It had come to Beeler's mind that there might be some of the Quineys they hadn't heard of for a long time out here in Arizona Territory, too. The sheriff might have heard of one or two of them. Why get them in hot water? Kin had to stick with kin.

Beeler met Graber and Leo in the middle of the street and showed them the money. Then she told the story of Mrs. Travis and all the insults to her and her critter, ending up with, "I surely feel sorry for that poor galoot who married with her."

Nate nodded. "I suspect he needs the comfort of saloons even if he's rich enough to own half of the businesses here. The postmaster told Leo and me some things about Mr. Travis."

"Uh-huh," came from Leo. "He said poor old man Travis has the look of a dyin' calf in a snowstorm on his face all the time."

Beeler pocketed the gold piece again. It was hers and Travis's. But she'd spend it if the three of them needed it.

"Did you find out where Sundown is, Nate?" she asked.

"Not exactly. But a saloon lady said she thought she recalled five men, 'funny lookers,' she claimed, a couple of months back. She said they were all shapes and sizes. They didn't drink much—though a couple of them gambled. One of them was wearing Mexican type spurs with big rowels. Another one was bald."

"He was truly bald," added Leo. "She said his head was so scalped of hair that when he took off his hat to her it looked like the moon was risin' up out of a line of hills."

Beeler rode over Nate's sound of annoyance. "That musta been them all right! Where'd they go?"

Nate answered, "The saloon lady didn't know, but when I asked at the post office, I turned up a Sunvale in this territory. It just got started as a town."

"Whereabouts in Arizona Territory?" asked Beeler.

"Well, the postmaster didn't know. It isn't in his book of post offices yet. He heard about it from somebody passing through here last week. He encourages travelers to drop in and tell him the names of new places. It keeps him up on things. When we find Sundown, he wants me to write him a letter and tell him where it is."

Beeler leaned against Travis, looking down at her wearing-out pants. She guessed maybe she did smell a bit high. She knew Leo did. Nate was examining his duds too. Even the Mexican leather looked scuffed and shabby. He said, "Let's mount up before Mrs. Travis sends somebody to see that we do leave. But that isn't the only reason I want to get going! There was a sign behind the bar in two saloons."

"What'd it say?" asked Beeler.

"I memorized it. It said, 'Gents will please leave their six-shooters behind the bar while in town. This will lessen the customary collection for burials.' "

"Well, did they leave 'em?" Beeler demanded.

"No, they didn't—not a lot of those I saw. That's the trouble."

Beeler nodded. She looked up at a sky that didn't have one cloud in it. "How many more miles do you suppose it's goin' to be to Sundown?"

8 MISS MUFFET

Riding west into Arizona Territory gave Beeler
more of a sinking feeling. They were still pretty
high up in canyon country, surrounded by caves that
might have bears in them. The pines and scrub oaks
didn't help much, even if they were green, because
they could hide wild animals and wilder folks. It was
closed-in land, scarey for prairie people. Some of the
rocks around this part of the country were as black as
Travis's hide, lava from old volcanoes, Nate explained.
Crossing them on horseback was a slipping and sliding
business, and when you looked up from these rocks
just as often as not your eye had to look at more, piled
up on top of each other as if somebody loco had tried
to build something. Beeler reckoned the Almighty
must have got weary of work and turned careless when
he made this part of the world and thrown it together
any which way out of what was left over from better
parts.

Worse, there was never one horsebacker in sight to tell them where Sundown might be—nobody at all. It made a person want to pull her bedroll over closer to somebody else's at night when the coyotes yowled— even if the somebody was Leo Quiney.

Beeler reckoned she felt some better about him, though. He'd done fine when the Apaches visited the circus, and he hadn't done anything out of line in the town of Travis. He looked to be improving. Beeler even told him one night while she was bashing up coffee beans for boiling with the butt of her six- shooter, "You ain't the raw product you was when we headed out from home."

He'd turned to Nate with a make-believe scowl on his face. "You hear that, Graber? She's said two kind words to me now. Didn't you think she done good, too, at times?"

Nate had laughed but only said "Yes." Beeler had kept an eye on him when he wasn't looking. He was thinning down now for sure, dropping tallow all the time. And his hair was yellow curls all over his head but not quite to the bottoms of his ears yet. It became him, losing lard and having curls, though she hoped he'd never get to the point Leo was—thin enough to split a hailstone. As for herself, her pants were getting looser every day. She was moving up onto the last notch of her belt.

The chance never came to ask Graber what he'd meant by unrequited love and that "maybe." But she'd keep on bearing it in mind, and someday she and he would ride over that same trail again.

When it came to trails, the one through these mountains wasn't easy to follow because it seemed not enough folks had traveled it to mark it well. In some places, especially over the black rocks, and there were whole acres of them in spots, the trail got lost. That's when the three of them fanned out and looked for sign of a trail leading west.

The afternoon of the second day out from the town of Travis, Beeler was afoot leading Jinglebob over the slick lava. She was hunting northwest, past the mouth of another canyon. Nate was searching due west and Leo southwest.

All at once Travis, who was behind Jinglebob, let out a snort and started to run, streaking by Beeler. Jinglebob reared up nickering. Beeler jerked out her six-shooter, then let go of the reins so Jinglebob could clatter off over the rocks after the longhorn. It must be a bear or a panther for sure! She let out a yell for the others. They'd come riding fast with Winchesters. Her eyes scanned the mouth of the canyon for some big animal watching her, but she couldn't spy any. There wasn't a wild thing in sight at the moment.

But as she stood her ground, her pistol ready, something did show up from behind some small rocks. It was walking mighty heavy for its size. The noise it made was what had spooked Jinglebob and Travis. The animal was white and black and pretty to look at —if you didn't know what it was. A skunk!

There wasn't anything more deadly to beast or man. A skunk was the scariest thing a person could run into. Not because of its stink, which was plenty bad enough, but because sometimes it had a disease called hydrophobia. It could be rabid. In Texas rabid skunks had been known to sneak into a man's bedroll with him and bite him. And he'd go loco and be a danger to everybody around him—gone pure brute himself. There wasn't any saving a person with hydrophobia. Being bit by a skunk that had it was as sure a death as being sentenced to hang by order of an Arkansas judge. Only a lot slower and more painful.

Her hands so shaky that she had to aim the six-shooter with both of them, Beeler drew a bead on the skunk. It was coming straight on toward her, waddling its way, rattling pebbles because it walked so heavily. That wasn't a natural thing for any wild animal to do, coming right up to her, so it must be sick. Wishing she had a shotgun to blow it apart, Beeler cocked the pistol.

But before she could pull the trigger, she heard a kid yelling from somewhere. It was too young a voice to be Nate or Leo. This was a weaner's voice. And now she saw the kid, a raggedy-looking little girl not more than five years old, coming on the run behind the skunk.

"Señorita Mofeta!" she squealed.

"Get back, I'm gonna shoot!" Beeler called out to her.

The child stopped dead still in her tracks. Her stare went from the skunk to the pistol. Suddenly she shrieked, "No, *señor*." To Beeler's horror the dark-haired child ran forward, scooped the skunk up in her arms, and buried her face in the animal's fur.

Beeler hung onto the pistol, trembling by now as if she had Saint Vitus Dance. And then Nate showed up on Stupid. He took in the whole trouble in one look. "My God," was what he said. Then he came out with fast words in Spanish. Beeler guessed he was telling the girl to put the skunk down. But she hung onto it.

Her head jerked up, and she talked back to Nate. After she was done, Beeler heard Nate sighing with relief. "It's all right," he said to her. "Put away the pistol, but let me uncock it for you first." As Beeler handed the pistol over to him, Nate told her, "The girl says she's María Lopez. The skunk is Señorita Mofeta. She doesn't have hydrophobia." He laughed. "She's María's pet. Would you believe it—a child's pet?"

Her hand still trembling so she rammed herself with
the six-shooter as she put it back into her belt, Beeler
asked, "Where'd them two come from?"

Nate talked some more in Spanish. "Back in the
canyon. María lives with her brother, father, and
grandmother."

"Why'd they live way out here?"

"Let me ask her."

Nate went on in Spanish again. Then he said,
"There's a mine back there. María's worried that the
señor with the long red hair will shoot Señorita Mofeta.
She means you."

Leo was beside them now and heard both Beeler
and Nate laughing. "What's goin' on?" he asked. He
took a gander at María Lopez and the skunk and
reined Two Cents around, ready to get out of there
pronto.

"Come back, Leo," Nate called to him. "The skunk's
a pet. She's healthy. The little girl says she doesn't
do what skunks generally do."

"How come the skunk don't?" Beeler wanted to
know.

"María says Señorita Mofeta thinks she's a cat."

Beeler's jaw dropped halfway to her brisket. "How
come a skunk'd think that?"

"She's been raised by the Lopez family. I ran into
this once before in Old Mexico. A skunk's death on

mice and pack rats and all other kinds of vermin. A real cat wouldn't last a week out here among the coyotes and mountain lions."

"I reckon that'd be true," granted Beeler.

"It is true. A skunk hasn't any real enemies."

"It hasn't got any real friends neither," said Beeler. "Nate, please tell that little gal I ain't a señor no more'n she is and I won't shoot her pet." She lifted her hat while Graber talked to María.

María seemed embarrassed. She came forward, still carrying the skunk, and stared into Beeler's face. She said, *"Lo siento mucho, señorita."* Then to Nate she added, *"La gringa salada es simpatica."*

"What'd she say?" asked Beeler.

"That she's very sorry she thought you were a boy and that the frog with freckles of an American girl is nice."

"Frog?" exploded Beeler. "I guess we can be on our way. Leo, go round up Jinglebob and my critter for me."

She turned away, but the little Mexican girl pulled at her arm, dragging her hand down into the skunk's fur. Beeler petted it nervously even if the fur was plenty soft. María said something more.

Whatever she said got Nate off Stupid in a hurry. "She wants us to come see her grandmother. She says she likes company. She wants to feed us."

María Lopez looked over her shoulder past Señorita Mofeta's head, then led the way into the canyon.

Nate told Beeler, "All you have to do is act *simpatica.*"

"For a good feed I reckon I can do it for a while at least. Mebbe Leo can, too, as soon as he gets my animals."

The Lopez family lived in a house that looked to be made of old boards nobody had wanted to throw away. It was close by a square black hole cut in the side of the canyon. A sure-enough mine, Beeler told herself.

A boy, larger than María, came out of the mine pushing a wheelbarrow. María shouted at him, "Matias," and the boy dropped the handles of the barrow to stare. Matias called out something in Spanish. The door of the shack opened, and in it stood a gray-headed woman wih a shotgun. Beeler and Nate stopped still.

María called out to her, holding up Señorita Mofeta. Then, tucking the skunk under her arm, she gestured toward the Texans. The old lady put down the shotgun. "María, put Miss Muffet down now that you've found her," she told the child in English.

The old lady came up to Beeler and Nate. She said, "How do you do?"

"Very well, thank you," came from Nate, who introduced himself and Beeler, and then added that Leo was on his way too.

The old lady's eyes were the light blue of Nerissa's prized forget-me-nots, though her face was as wrinkled as a burned boot. She wasn't any Mexican—not with those blue eyes and talking English so well.

Beeler just had to know. "How come you talk English to us and Spanish to them two kids?"

"Because I speak both languages. I'm Señora Mary Rose Seton de Lopez. I was born and reared in Galveston." She shook Beeler's hand, cracking the girl's knuckles. Then she shook Nate's.

"Light a spell," she told the Texans. "We'll be eatin' pretty soon. I know we look to be so poor we don't even own a name, but we set a pretty good table."

Nate accepted for both of them, then asked, "Do you know where a town named Sunset or Sundown would be—or a place called Sunvale? My father might be there."

"They must be new places. I don't know of them. I've been sitting on top of a silver mine for two years now. I'm a widow woman. My son, Pedro, rode off to town with some ore samples to the assay office three days ago. If you're about to ask about the children's mother, she's dead. She died a year after María was born. That child's a trial to me. I try to teach her and Matias, but all they want to do is chase that skunk and hack away at a vein of silver. I want them to know their ABC's and how to figure numbers so they'll be ready for school when Pedro and I leave here."

A loud sound over the rock floor of the canyon made everybody turn around. There was Leo, leading Jinglebob and holding Travis's neck rope. Beeler watched him. He put the end of the neck rope between his teeth and Jinglebob's reins in the same hand as Two Cents's and took off his hat to Señora Lopez. Beeler was disgusted, remembering Elfie Billywhiskers. That Leo could butter up womenfolks when he wanted to like nothing she'd ever seen. But he only buttered up stranger ladies. He'd never took the trouble to brighten her life or Nerissa's.

Señora Lopez handed the shotgun to Beeler and went up to Travis. He let her pat him and then she patted Jinglebob. When she came back, she said, "There's some hay and oats here for your animals back of the shack. That steer's getting to be mostly legs and horns. It's a pitiful pass he's come to."

"We rode a long ways from Santa Rosa County, Texas. So has he," Beeler apologized for Travis.

"And you all sure look it," agreed the old lady. "I'll hunt up a needle and thread to patch your britches. Then you can tell me what brings you out here in the wilds. I bet it's a good story."

Beeler whispered to Nate, after Leo had dismounted and gone with Matias to lead the horses away, "Ask the Missus what brought her out here and why she's got herself tied up with Mexicans."

He spoke fiercely to her. "I'll ask her why she's in Arizona Territory—but not about Mexicans. Mexicans have very good manners. They wouldn't ever have asked her husband why he married a woman from Texas!"

Beeler fell in step with Graber. "But I'll bet you some Mexicans wondered."

He gave her a look that said "Wilt," but she wouldn't give him that satisfaction. "I wouldn't be at all surprised that they did wonder," he hissed.

The shack was as miserable inside as on the outside. It had a table and rickety chairs and two bunk beds only. It seemed clear that the Lopez children slept on the floor. The only valuable things in the place were the one glass window in the back wall and a large black cookstove. Something in a pot was on it cooling, and whatever it was smelled just fine to Beeler.

Señora Lopez waved her hand at the Texans to take a seat. Just as Beeler got comfortable, thinking how long it'd been since her backside had felt a chair, there came a scratching at the door.

"Let Miss Muffet in, please," the old lady ordered Leo, who was closest to the door.

He got up and opened it and in came the skunk. She walked straight over to a bowl in a corner. "That's a good puss," said the old lady.

Beeler asked, "Why do you call her Miss Muffet?"

"Because when she was just a baby abandoned by her maw, I used to feed her on curds and whey. Does that answer you, honey?"

"It oughta," came from Leo. "Beeler used to carry many a bucket of milk to that steer of hers when it was little."

"Yes, it answers her question," said Nate, kicking Beeler under the table.

"Why're you kickin' me, Graber? What'd I do that was bad?" Beeler demanded.

"You started in asking questions," he whispered.

Beeler glared at him but kept quiet. There was no stopping Leo, though. "Can Miss Muffet do what other skunks do, Missus Lopez?"

"Far as we know, she can, but she's much too well-trained. And by disposition Miss Muffet's mighty polite."

Later on Señora Lopez gave them and her grand-children a bowl of chili beans that tasted better than any Beeler had ever had before. The old lady served fresh fried doughnuts with them, first cutting out the holes for the skunk to eat. Miss Muffet wanted out the minute she'd gulped down the raw dough. After-wards the old woman took up some knitting out of a basket and said, "Of course, you're wondering what brought me out here in the middle of nowhere."

"We surely are, ma'am," came from Beeler, as she jerked her foot away from Nate's boot.

"Well, I came out here as a bride, married to Mr. Terwilliger." She sighed. "We left damp Galveston because of his health. He lived on egg yolks beaten with potatoes and water for a whole year at one time. It was all his stomach would stomach. We had the Hog's Eye Basin Ranch until he died. Then I clerked in a little trading post until I met Mr. Aitken and married up with him. We had a ranch, too. It was a mighty pretty place. I had a flower garden. I took snuff then and saved all them little bottles to make borders for my flower beds. Then Mr. Aitken died, too. He died with a bottle in his hand and a bottle inside. He was never destined to die of thirst." She dropped a stitch, muttered some, then picked it up. "Next time around I married Señor Lopez. He was Mexican. We had some fine times at fandangos in town before he died. We used to take our son to them when he was your age, Leo, and Señor Lopez was still alive. Have you ever been to a fandango?"

"Yes," said Nate.

"No," said Beeler and Leo.

"Well, the floorboards are greased slick with tallow for the dancing. And such music from the accordion and fiddler—not to mention the guitars! Mexican guitars. Señor Lopez was a fine dancer. He died right in the middle of the floor."

Beeler thought this shack was a far place from fandangos. She felt mighty sorry for the lady who'd had three husbands. "But how come you left town?" she asked. "I guess you musta lived near one?"

"Our son wanted to be a miner, not a rancher, so we sold the spread when his wife died. He built this shack so we can live here and guard the mine."

Leo put in, "It must have plenty of silver in it."

"It has some. That's why I met you with a shotgun."

"We ain't thieves," volunteered Beeler. After a stabbing look at Leo, she added, "Leastwise not silver thieves."

"I didn't reckon you were. All the same I do a lot of worrying. That was good ore my son took to town with him, and the word gets around a place fast when samples are good. I'll be glad when he gets back and we leave here. He's thinking of selling the mine. I want to move back to civilization—or what Arizona Territory calls civilization. It surely isn't Galveston. I want to talk English more than I do. Spanish is a mighty pretty language, but all the same I like to talk English at times. Sort of to keep my hand in I write to my sister whenever I can. She lives in Houston. Do you write to your kin, Beulah Land?"

Beeler felt herself turning red in the face. For a fact, she'd been around some post offices since she'd left Cottonwood, but she hadn't thought to write Nerissa. "I didn't ever have no paper or pen, ma'am."

"A poor excuse," grunted the old lady. "To get a letter a body has to write one. I write some, and I get some. Riders coming over the trail from Bartlett fetch me letters. There are two things I'm always glad to see out here—the peddler's wagon and somebody bringing a letter."

"When we find Sundown, I'll try to write from there," promised Beeler.

The rest of that afternoon Beeler spent in the shack. Matias took Nate and Leo into the mine but wouldn't let Beeler come too. Women in a mine made for bad luck, Señora Lopez told her after they'd gone. The old lady laughed. "Dumbest thing I ever heard tell. I went in there once when they were all out of sight. There was nothing to see but rocks. Nothing bad happened, but I never let 'em know I went in. I humor men, not fight 'em."

"That ain't *my* way. I won't jolly 'em along when they're bein' stupid," Beeler spat.

"Suit yourself, honey."

That night the Quineys and Nate spread their bedrolls on the floor next to the Lopez children's blankets. María and Matias chatted in fast Spanish with Nate and in very slow English with the Quineys. Their grandmother was trying to teach them English when she could catch them. Catching María was the hardest.

She preferred chasing Miss Muffet up and down the canyon. When the skunk wanted out that night and scratched at the door, María whimpered. She wanted to sleep with the animal. Beeler was relieved when Matias got up and let the skunk out into the night.

Breakfast at the Lopez's wasn't Mexican style. It was sourdough pancakes and molasses and good coffee. Beeler hated to leave and so did the boys, but they had to. Señora Lopez had sewed up the tears in their clothes and the horses had been fed and had a rest. They were just about to say *gracias* and *adiós,* and Beeler was wishing she had a farewell present to give María, when they heard the sound of hoofbeats on the canyon floor.

"Papa," shouted María and raced ahead and around a boulder. She came running back just as fast, calling out, *"Hombre, hombre!"* this time.

Beeler felt for the pistol while Nate and Leo readied their Winchesters. With all this artillery around, Señora Lopez still went into the shack for the shotgun.

The man who came riding in on a chunky sorrel had a yellow mustache and beard streaked with tobacco stains. When he saw the guns trained on him, he put his hands in the air. He smiled and said, "If you're Missus Lopez, I brung a letter for ya from Bartlett."

"Who's it from?" she asked.

The rider shook his head. "I can't read, so how'd I be able to tell? The postmaster in town, he give it to me because I was ridin' this way and knowed where this canyon is. He said the letter was from someplace in Texas, though."

"All right, get down, and come on in and have some coffee. I'm expecting a letter from Texas." The old woman lowered the shotgun. "You come back, too," she told the Quineys and Nate. "It'll be from my sister, Nora, and I might want to reply to it right off. You can carry it with you and mail it for me in the next town you come to."

"We'd be honored to do that," said Nate, as Matias came up with their horses, Travis trailing them. Nate and Leo put the Winchesters into the saddle scabbards while Beeler stuffed the six-shooter back under her left ribs. They followed the stranger into the shack while Matias took the horses and Travis back of the shack once more. Beeler guessed she knew why. Miss Muffet was loose. She hadn't come in that morning yet at all. Once the horses and longhorn spotted her, there'd be no holding them.

The stranger sat down at the table without taking off his hat. He waited until Señora Lopez had poured him a mug of coffee and more coffee for the Texans. María and Matias, curious about the letter, came inside, too, to stand against the wall. The man reached his hand into his vest pocket.

Out came a derringer, a little bitty one, instead of an envelope. Beeler caught her breath. At short range a derringer could kill a person easy.

"Don't anyone of ya say a word," he warned. "I heard tell in Bartlett that this mine's got lotsa high-grade ore in it. I have it in mind to take a sack of it with me wherever I'm goin'."

Señora Lopez said calmly, "My son isn't here to get it for you."

"I know it. I seen him in town, braggin' in the assay office."

"There isn't anybody to dig out the ore here. It isn't easy work," said the old woman.

"Ain't there? How about them three boys and the biggest Mex kid?" The stranger jerked his head at the Texans and Matias Lopez.

"We won't do it!" said Nate, surprising Beeler.

"Look, sonny boy, I don't want to have to shoot anybody. But if I have to shoot one, I'll do it right where his galluses cross to get the others workin'."

"I ain't a he like them," Beeler put in hastily.

"No matter. You're big enough to swing a pickaxe."

For a while there was dead silence with everybody staring at the robber. Beeler was just about to say that it was bad luck to have womenfolks in a mine, but as she opened her mouth there was a scratching at the door.

The high-grader didn't turn his head to look at the

door. He asked from where he sat, "What's that there?" Other words came out of Beeler. "It's Miss Muffet. She's been out all night."

Señora Lopez put in real fast before the man could say anything. "Lands sake, Beulah Land, let her in before she sets up that awful yowling. She's probably caught a mouse and wants to show it to us. Let her in, and then you can go to the mine."

Beeler moved to the door. She opened it, held her breath, and called, "Here kitty, kitty, kitty."

In tromped the skunk without looking either to the right or the left. She paraded right over to her bowl in the corner as though she never even saw the high-grader.

He saw Miss Muffet, though. He let out the wildest yell Beeler had ever heard, dropped the derringer, ran for the window, and jumped through it, glass and all. Headfirst, he went.

Leo was standing over him with the shotgun before he could get up. Beeler was behind him with the six-shooter and Nate with the derringer. Nate and Leo hog-tied the man, who was cut up around the face and hands by the glass. Then Nate gave the derringer to Señora Lopez while María and Matias watched, big-eyed beside their smiling grandmother.

"He'll stay tied up that way until my son gets here. Then Pedro'll take him to justice," she told the Texans.

Nate and Leo had their backs turned while they conferred with the old lady on how long it'd be before she thought Pedro would return, so Beeler snuck into the mine for a quick look-see. Nobody had eyes now for her—only for the scowling tied-up high-grader. The mine disappointed Beeler. Señora Lopez had been right as rain. There wasn't anything to see but some wood shoring and some pale gray streaks in the rock wall.

After the Texans said *adiós* for the second time and mounted up, Beeler did some pondering. Travel was really only interesting when there was something interesting to look at.

Menfolks could keep their old mines from now on. From the way Nate described them once on the trail, one tunnel-type mine was pretty much like another. Once you'd seen one, you'd seen them all.

9 MAJOR GORDON

Señora Lopez had given them good instructions on how to find Bartlett, but as they rode farther west Beeler was uneasy again. Because the town was out on the desert, the woman had even told them how to travel there. By night! By day it would be hot enough to sizzle a horned frog. They'd have to carry enough water for themselves and their animals. In a pinch Travis could get water out of prickly pear cactus, but the horses weren't that talented. Señora Lopez had told them about the special kind of cactus that looked like a green barrel, in case they ran real low on water. It had water inside. Mesquite anywhere meant water not far off. She warned them, too, about all the dangerous biting things on the desert—oversize hairy spiders, rattlesnakes, and poison lizards.

Nate told the Quineys the first night they camped that he'd traveled in the desert before, in Old Mexico. He knew how to get around in sand country, but he had let Señora Lopez talk. She was getting practice in English and that was what she wanted. Still and all, even if Graber knew about dry country, Beeler wasn't boiling over with eagerness to ride through it.

Sleeping for two days in the shade of rocks away from a scorching sun and sky too bright blue for eye comfort and riding two nights under a sky glitter-white with stars brought them finally to Bartlett. At sunrise they came through a gravelly countryside dotted with greasewood and prickly pear, and there it was—Bartlett. It was mostly an adobe town set on a riverbank fairly close to some more mountains, which was to be expected in this country where you weren't ever really out of sight of them. What was surprising, though, was that the railroad was here—so far west.

Once more Travis, Two Cents, and Stupid had to be led over the gleaming new tracks. Critters for the most part just didn't take to unnatural sights. Jinglebob didn't kick up one bit of fuss this time, though. He stepped carefully over the tracks with Beeler still on his back. She was mighty proud of him, although how he'd act if he ever saw a locomotive was anybody's guess. But there wasn't a train or engine in sight here in Bartlett—only a lonely-looking depot. That wouldn't spook any horse.

They found one man out so early walking up the center of Bartlett's street. He was sober enough to tell them that he hadn't heard of Sundown or Sunset or even of Sunvale, but then he'd only been in Bartlett for six weeks. Bartlett was just a railhead town for a bigger, older place a distance away, Hard Rock. It had been set up in 1879, a couple of years back. He said it had seven thousand folks, elegant cafés where you could eat lobster brought by fast stagecoach from the Gulf of Mexico, and a real live theater where world-famous players came. If anybody had any idea where Sunvale or those other places were, it would be the postmaster of Hard Rock! It was one of the most important towns in Arizona Territory—and close to gold fields.

"Is Hard Rock a very rough town?" Nate had asked him.

"Sure is, son," had been the reply. "But there's a Law and Order Society there, and there's a sheriff and whole family of brothers workin' with the U.S. Marshal. And,"—the man laughed—"there's Major Gordon."

"Is he part of the U.S. Army?" Nate asked.

"No, but Major Gordon's a whole force alone, let me tell you. You look up the Major the minute you get in town, and you'll be helped. Lord, will you ever be taken care of!"

Three hours riding south, in the cool of the morning

through miles of seven-foot-tall yucca plants, brought them to Hard Rock. It was a desert place, like Bartlett, but set on hills covered with cactus and it had more than one street. The Quineys and Nate gawked plenty as they rode up the main street. There were some fancy buildings here. Some of them were saloons and gambling houses; others were cafés. Piano music came spilling out of a swinging-door place that was the most oversized saloon Beeler had ever set eyes on. It was made of wood and even had paint on it, a nice gray shade. Hard Rock had three of the biggest adobe houses she'd ever seen. One was a theater, another a boardinghouse-hotel, and the third one a church with a wooden steeple on top. As they read signs looking for the post office, Beeler took note that Hard Rock had a newspaper, *The Nugget.* It had doctors and lawyers and even dentists, which was more than Cottonwood had—dentists.

But judging from the men they saw, it had its hair on all the same. Some of them had rough-looking, mean faces even if they were dolled up in fancy frock coats and more than likely weren't anything more than porch-perching dudes.

They surely stared at Travis as if they'd never seen a Texas longhorn before. One man in a plug hat shouted out, "Hey, look, them kids brought their beef with 'em!"

"He's jerky on the hoof," a velvet-collared galoot across the street called back.

Beeler told her critter beside her, "Never you mind them. You've thinned down some. They haven't come half so far as you and me, Travis. If they did, they wouldn't run so much to lard as they do."

The post office showed up finally along the street. Nate dismounted and tethered Stupid to the hitching rail out front. Neither of the Quineys went inside with him. They were surrounded by a crowd of kids.

A small girl with long, straight, corn-colored hair, a sunburned nose, and round green-brown eyes stood nearest to Travis. Her dress was rose-colored calico, her sunbonnet dangling by its strings. She spoke to Beeler, pointing to the steer, "What's his name, Mister?"

"I ain't a mister. His name's Travis."

"Where'd you come from?"

"From Santa Rosa County, Texas," Beeler told her. Then the two girls howdied and shook. "I'm Beulah Land Quiney. This is my brother, Leo."

The girl grinned. "I'm Lorena." She eyed Travis some more, then went around to shake Leo's hand too. "Why'd you come to Hard Rock?" she asked.

"We're huntin' some folks," said Leo.

Nate came out before Lorena could ask any more questions. Beeler thought he looked to be sagging. She guessed by the expression on his face he hadn't had any luck finding Sundown again. "Well, did ya find out where Sunvale or them others is?"

"No, the postmaster never heard of any one of them."

"Shall we start lookin', and askin' in the saloons again?" Leo was halfway off Two Cents.

Lorena piped up. "Oh, you better not go in saloons. It'll get you in trouble here. I looked under the door of the Glass Palace once to see the pretty mirrors and got thrashed for it. By the saloon owner—not by her."

"Who's her?" asked Nate. "Your mother?"

"Oh, no! Major Gordon. I'm an orphan. I live at her house."

"Is it an orphanage?" Nate wanted to know.

"It's a lot of things. A boardinghouse and hospital and a hotel. Major Gordon runs it."

"A *lady* major?" asked Nate.

Lorena giggled. "It's what folks here in Hard Rock nicknamed her. She's really Ella Gordon. She ain't married. Come on home with me. You'll get tossed out of saloons here. Maybe she can help you out."

Nate shook his head, but Beeler spoke to him. "Remember what the galoot in Bartlett said. Major Gordon's a people helper."

"All right, Beulah Land." Nate hauled himself back onto Stupid. "Lead the way, please," he told Lorena.

Lorena ran ahead of them, her hair flying, until they came to the big adobe hotel they'd already noticed. She ran inside yelling before the Texans came to a halt.

A minute later someone came out onto the wooden porch with a broom in her hand. It was a lady wearing a pair of overalls and man's shirt. Over the overalls was a yellow calico apron. She had thick dark hair piled up in a knot on top of her head, a sunburned face, and spectacles.

Lorena came right behind her, smiling and pointing. "That's them, ma'am, the ones I was telling you about. The cow's name is Travis. He's from Texas."

Major Ella had sort of a deep voice for a lady and had a queer sort of accent, not Mexican, but a bit blurry. "Good Lord," Beeler heard her exclaim. "They look like the work of a Kansas cyclone."

Nate took off his hat and so did Leo. Then Nate introduced them all and explained his errand and asked his usual question.

The woman shook her head. "I don't know of the town, I'm sorry to say. Are you hungry?"

"Hungrier than a woodpecker with a big headache," came from Leo.

"We can pay you," said Nate.

"There'll be no charge," said Major Ella, "on one condition. You must all have a bath before lunch."

A bath! Beeler was horrified. "We haven't any clean duds."

Major Ella came closer and removed her spectacles. "Why, you're a girl!"

"Yes'm. Beulah Land's a girl name in Texas. The pants fool a lot a folks."

This made the woman smile. "Don't pay those folks any heed. There's nothing as practical as trousers. I wear skirts to church and that's the only place. Now take the horses behind the house and give them to Doyle. He'll stable the poor things."

"What about my steer?" asked Beeler.

"Tell Mitchell to tie him somewhere out of the sun where he won't be in anyone's way. Mitchell will see that he has water and hay. He needs some beef on his bones."

Doyle turned out to be a yellow-headed boy, a frying-size kid, and Lorena's brother. Mitchell, no kin to her, was Leo's age, brown haired, brown eyed, and muscular. With Beeler helping him, he tied Travis to the crossbar of a clothesline.

"What's this Major Ella like?" Beeler heard Leo asking him. "She wants us to take a bath."

Mitchell looked mournful as he said, "She comes from Scotland. They must be awful clean over there. The Major's fine in character, but she thinks soap and water will cure anything."

"I ain't gonna grow up and be like that," Beeler exploded.

"Tiger cat, ain't you?" asked Mitchell with a sly smile. "Well, let me tell ya, Major Ella's gettin' the water and towels ready right now."

"She makes us wash all over every week," came from small Doyle. "Sometimes when we get dirty, it's oftener than that." He looked mournful too as he spoke.

Beeler had the first bath. The instant she was into the tub, Lorena knocked on the door, popped in, scooped up all of Beeler's clothes, and started out again. She left the gold pieces behind.

"What're you up to?" yelled Beeler.

"Washing your clothes. The washboard and the Major are ready. She says in this sun by the time you've washed your hair, too, your clothes will be almost dry. I'll fetch you a wrapper of hers."

"Where's my brother and Graber?"

"Waiting in line for the tub. Hurry up."

Beeler scrubbed, noticing how the water got browner and browner as she shed Texas and New Mexico Territory. Finally it looked like a Texas river in the springtime. Once she was out and into the striped flannel wrapper Lorena brought her, she reckoned she was a pound lighter and a ton weaker. She waited in Lorena's little room playing seven-card stud poker with her, with deuces and one-eyed jacks wild, until her clothes were dry.

Lorena listened carefully to what folks said. She thought Beeler had lots of grit to come after Jinglebob the way she did and all the way to Hard Rock too.

"Well, it wasn't exactly that. It's come to be a bit more with me." Beeler looked at the jack of diamonds in her hand, thinking of Nate. Leo had stuck like glue lately. There hadn't been one chance to ask Nate again what he'd meant by that "maybe" or about unrequited love. Those Apaches might have done the bicyclienne and lion tamer some good, but they hadn't done her any. They'd picked the wrong minute to show up for sure.

After a lunch of roast-beef hash the Quineys and Graber had more chance to see how Major Ella came by her nickname. She'd already locked up their Winchesters and six-shooter before she'd made them take baths. Now she even had Leo in a new shirt. He and Nate were a mite paler, Beeler noted.

Major Ella, her orphans, and the Texans sat at a round table in one corner of her dining room. She wouldn't let anyone say a word until they'd eaten everything on their plates, which wasn't hard to do because the grub was good. She told them, "Chatted food is half-digested food. We'll talk later."

After lunch she jumped straight to the point—first about their problem finding Nate's pa and then about Travis. She said, "The editor of *The Nugget,* our

newspaper, eats supper here because I consider his
stomach. He doesn't like the fancy fluff duffs served at
the local cafés. I'll tell Mr. Hays about your quest
tonight, and he'll make an appeal in the paper for any
information about Sundown or Sunset or Sunvale.
Everybody in Hard Rock reads *The Nugget*. It's a
weekly, but it comes out day after tomorrow."

"Thank you," said Nate.

Major Ella was brisk. "If nobody comes forward,
I'd advise the three of you to abandon the whole enter-
prise. Stay here for a time and let your animals re-
cuperate and then go back to Texas."

Nate sighed. "I guess you're right, ma'am."

"I am right, young man." The woman turned to
Beeler. "Now about that longhorn of yours. My clothesline won't hold him. He's already pulled loose and run
under a laundry. He ate your brother's shirt even if it
had been washed. You know how grass eaters crave
something salty. He took the sheets down into the dust
as well, so they had to be rinsed over again. He was so
fouled up in clothesline Mitchell had to cut him free.
My solution is for the steer to have the run of Hard
Rock."

Beeler leaped up. "Somebody'll shoot him!"

"No, they won't. There will be mention of him in
the newspaper also. But he must have some sort of
easily visible distinguishing mark."

"He has," said Leo. "Big horns for his age."

"No, no!" Major Ella waved her hand, brushing away Leo's comment. "I mean something truly spectacular. I favor a ribbon on one horn and another on his tail. That would mark him out just fine as a child's pet."

Beeler sat down. Travis decked out in ribbons? "How about a sign on him?" she said, thinking of the chariot horses.

"No, he could lean against something and rub that off. The ribbons will do the trick. And they will not hamper his movements."

"How long'll it be before we hear from somebody who might read about us in the newspaper?" asked Beeler.

"We'd best give it a week."

Beeler pulled the gold double eagle out of her pocket and gave it to Major Ella, who gave it right back.

"No money is required. You will work for your room and board. I have found a job for you, Jonathan, in the general store. The owner has supper here too. You will sweep the floors, clean and fill the oil lamps, and dust the counters. I'll collect your wages. Leo, you will help Mitchell and Doyle in the stables and do odd jobs I require. You, Beulah Land, will help in the kitchen and wait on table. And keep out of the sun. All it does for women here is make them shrivel up."

"I don't know how to wait on tables," protested Beeler.

"It's a simple process. Keep your hands clean, your mouth shut. Serve plates from the left and take away from the right. That is all there is to it. Everyone eats the same victuals."

Beeler felt defeat. She'd met her match—someone more set in her ways than Nerissa was. She hoped there'd be some results from the newspaper piece fast.

Major Gordon was finished with them now and was dictating a grocery list to Lorena, who always wore a pencil on a string around her neck when she was in the house. "Tell that clerk at the general store that I need a tub of lard, a crock of apple butter, and two loaves of sugar."

Quick as a flash, she turned back to the Texans. "Tonight we'll take in an early candlelight revivalist service. It's in a tent. You can go there, Beulah Land, in trousers." She clapped her hands. "Now off with you—every one of you. Beulah Land, clear the table, then ask the cook what you can do to help him. Jonathan, you go to the general store now with Lorena. She will introduce you. Leo, you go out with the boys and curry comb the horses that will permit you to work on them. And, Mitchell, once you've tied the ribbons to the steer, let him go."

Major Ella got up, went to a golden oak highboy,

opened a drawer, and took out two wide ribbons. One was pink. One was white. "These were to have been hair bows for your birthday, Lorena, but they'll have to be put to emergency use now."

"That's just fine, ma'am," said Lorena. She whispered to Beeler, "Your steer will look right pretty with the pink one on him. I'll ask Mitchell to put it on his horn, not his tail. Pink up close to the face is mighty becoming."

"Holy gatlins," muttered Leo, who'd heard Lorena. "It's enough to make a coyote hoot like an owl."

Mr. Howard Hays, a round-faced man with black curling hair and a black-and-white checkered frock coat, was the newspaper editor. He was mighty pleasant to Nate and the Quineys and even wrote down notes on the back of an envelope in his pocket about their travels. Beeler thought he seemed very interested. He said he'd spotted Travis moseying around town and been struck by the ribbons fluttering on him. He was even more struck to hear that Beeler could whistle him in whenever she had a mind to. Beeler liked Mr. Hays.

So did Major Ella for a fact. She let him talk at the table with them—whether it was because she favored him or because he was a "paying guest," Beeler didn't know.

"What will you call the article, Mr. Hays?" asked the woman, as she set a dish of "spotted pup," rice and raisins, in front of the editor.

"Texas Longhorn and His Young Owners Surrender to the Hospitality of Hard Rock."

"We ain't surrenderin' to anybody," came from Leo.

"It's only a manner of speaking, Leo. It will attract readers and that's what we want, isn't it?"

"Yes sir, it is!" said Nate, as he dug into his spotted pup too.

Mr. Hays did fine by them. There was even a drawing of Travis running around town. The article was on the front page, and it took care just dandy of people who might have in mind to shoot Travis for beef. Mr. Hays said in it that the steer was "under the protection of the town," that he was a "child's pet" and that anyone who harmed him in any way would surely be "prosecuted to the fullest extent of the law." Beeler hoped that the folks who could read would read it to them that couldn't—the way she did to Leo.

They waited for four days while Travis roamed loose, coming back now and then to rest on Major Ella's front porch and to get a handout from Mitchell. And then on the morning of the fifth day, the man and woman showed up. The woman was a bitty thing and

the man big, but you could tell right off who wore the
bell. She had crackling black eyes under her sunbonnet, and he wore a mournful look. She shoved the
Nugget article into Major Ella's hand. "We're the
Turners, Alfred and me. Alfred thinks he might know
something about this place, Sundown. Tell the Major
what you know, Alfred."

Alfred had a sheep's face. "Well, I ain't really sure,
lovey."

"Of course, you ain't, you son of barley corn," said
Mrs. Turner. She added to Major Ella, "Alfred's chief
interest in life up to a couple months ago was Forty
Rod."

Major Ella's lips tightened. "Kansas sheep dip! It's
certainly no product of Scotland, that stuff. Forty Rod
whiskey is made in Hard Rock and that explains much.
It rots a man's innards."

Before the ladies could talk about Forty Rod some
more, Nate put in, "Where is Sundown, Mr. Turner?"

Alfred let out a long mumble. "There's a Sundown
saloon on the California side of the Colorado at Gilaville."

"California or Colorado?" asked Nate. He looked
puzzled.

Major Gordon explained. "The Colorado River is
the boundary between Arizona Territory and California. Gilaville is a town in Arizona Territory."

"Sort of on both sides," put in Mr. Turner. "The Sundown saloon's next door to the Last Chance."

"The last chance to what?" asked Beeler.

"To wet your whistle before you get to San Diego out on the Pacific Ocean. San Diego's near three hundred miles across the desert. Them two saloons, the Sundown one and the Last Chance, are just about all there is on that side of the river. I know the area, because I've drove freight trains all over it. I been here since 1877."

Nate shook his head. "A saloon is the only place you know by that name, Mr. Turner?"

"It's all anybody knows."

"Alfred knows saloons!" said Mrs. Turner. She nodded to Major Ella, took her husband's arm, and left, leaving Nate looking more down at the mouth than Beeler had ever seen him. The idea that Sundown was a den of devilment wasn't appealing to him one bit.

"Now, Jonathan," said the Major, "saloon or no, you'll have to go there to satisfy your curiosity."

"Oh, I know that, but I don't want to."

"Nonsense. There is nothing so wretched to a body's peace of mind as unsatisfied curiosity."

Beeler felt her heart going out to Nate. His old whiskey soak of a pa in a saloon, not even a town. Poor cuss!

"I just don't want to get on that horse again," said

Nate. "They told me at the general store that it's all rattlesnakes and cactus west of here for hundreds of miles."

Major Ella snorted. "Who said anything about riding over that dreadful desert—which truly is nothing but lizards and scorpions and heat. You'll go by *train*! The horses and the longhorn will stay here and rest. Mitchell will hitch up my rig and drive you to Bartlett in the morning. There's a westbound passenger train going through there at noon."

Beeler watched Nate brighten up. She guessed he'd never set foot on a train either. "Are Leo and me goin' with you on a train too?" she asked Nate. Being a waiter-girl wasn't to her liking.

"In for a penny, in for a pound," he told her, sounding sad.

Leo wanted to know, "What does that mean?"

"Oh, you two will go all the way with me."

Beeler was glad she didn't have to convince Graber. She wanted to grab him and hug him but didn't in public. Instead she got him by the hand and hauled him out onto the front porch where Travis was standing blocking everybody's way, his ribbons blowing in the hot wind off the desert. Beeler wanted to call out to all of Hard Rock that they'd located a Sundown! But that would embarrass Nate. She hugged Travis around the neck and told him, "We found it."

Nate smiled weakly and put out a hand to pat the

steer on the flank. Travis looked mildly at him and for the first time showed some affection for him by shifting his weight and leaning toward him.

The trouble was that Nate didn't move his feet fast enough, the way Beeler had learned to. Travis's right hind foot came down on top of Nate's left foot. It only rested there for a second, but it was enough. Graber let out a howl that drove Travis down the street, taking out a porch post as he went. Nate grabbed his injured foot in both hands, hopping up and down on his good one, yelling all the time.

10 UNDER THE BRIDGE

Major Ella was on top of the trouble right away. She sent Mitchell for the doctor while Nate limped upstairs to his room. Beeler and Leo stood outside the door, waiting while the doctor looked at Nate's foot.

"It wasn't my critter's fault," Beeler told her brother for the third time.

The doctor wouldn't speak to the Quineys, though they tugged at his coat sleeves. But he talked with Major Ella, and when he did, the Texans heard him. "There are a couple of bones broken in that lad's foot. I've bandaged it."

"He's supposed to take the westbound train to Gilaville tomorrow," said the Major.

"That boy isn't going anywhere. He won't be able to get a boot on for some time. One thing you can say about being stepped on by a cow, it usually creates some damage!"

Beeler and Leo looked at one another. Graber *not* able to go now that they'd finally found a place called Sundown!

"I guess this is the end of our string, Beeler," said Leo. He turned his back on her, put his hands in his pockets, hunched up his shoulders, and walked off down the hallway.

Beeler didn't follow him. She opened Nate's door without knocking and went inside. Nate was flopped on the bed, his feet on a pillow. He looked at her. Then, not letting her get out one word about how sorry she was Travis had stepped on him, he yelled, "You and that damned animal of yours! Leave me alone! I don't ever want to see either of you again!"

"He's only a critter. He didn't mean to walk on you."

Graber reached under his head, grabbed the pillow, and threw it at her. "You're a critter, too. All of you Quineys are. You're mean enough to have a reserved seat in hell and as conceited as a barber's cat."

Beeler felt her feelings growing fiery. "There ain't no call to talk like that about Leo and me. We done plenty for you."

"I wish you hadn't. I must have been crazy to come to the ranch hunting for Quineys. You have to be the most stubborn and ornery people in all of Texas."

"No, we ain't. Don't forget, you're from Texas too. There are others I could lay tongue to. You wasn't so mad at us before you had this accident. You got a mean disposition." She put her hand on the doorknob. "And I was startin' to have tender feelings toward you."

"*Tender!*" Nate was screeching like an owl now. "You mash up my foot so I can't go to Sundown and you call that 'tender.' Do you think I could feel tender about you? You scare me half to death when you're not making me mad enough to explode. You don't even know enough not to ask a stranger his name." His face grew calmer, and he smiled in a mean way. "Besides, there's somebody else I feel tender towards."

Beeler froze. This was something different. Nate had been mad at Travis and was taking it out on her and Leo. She could understand his doing that. It was natural, and it'd pass. But another girl! "Who'd she be? Are you tellin' me Cupid's already throwed his rope on you?"

"He surely has. Her name is Bonnie Annie Laurie. She lives up on that wheat farm where I do. She reads books, plays the harp, and is as pretty as can be."

"Has she got blue eyes and yeller hair?"

"Yes. Bee trees are gall beside her."

Beeler opened the door and slammed it behind her. "No-good son of a goat," she said to herself, as she leaned against the door. She wondered how many sweethearts old Graber had staked out over Texas. Mad as a rooster caught in a rainstorm, Beeler tromped downstairs. Right now what she needed was a few kind words—but where to get them? She had to talk woman to woman, and Lorena wasn't one yet. There was hope, though, with Major Ella.

Fuming at the meanness of Graber, Beeler went outside behind the big adobe. That's where the cook said the Major would be. She was taking down laundry.

Beeler came straight out with it. "Graber, he just now told me he hasn't got any use for me. He says there's a yeller-headed gal in north Texas he favors."

Major Ella nodded. Through a clothespin in her mouth she said, "That's his privilege. What do you have in mind to do? Ride back there and shoot her?"

"It did come to mind. He told me he knew somethin' about unrequited love once. I thought mebbe he meant me."

"He must have meant the blond girl, Beulah Land."

"It must of been her." Suddenly Beeler felt some hope rising up yeasty in her. She snapped her fingers. "He favors her, but it looks like she don't favor him. Y' know, ma'am, he never wrote her one letter all the time we been gone." Suddenly she asked, "Major, have you ever felt tender toward somebody?"

The woman dropped a pillow case into the laundry basket before she answered. "In love you mean, don't you? Yes, I loved a man once enough to marry him. But for a couple of reasons I never did. Now that I look back on it, it was a good thing, too." She reached up for a towel, pulling off the clothespin. "If I had married him and had a big family, I'd have ended up doing things only for them for years and years, wouldn't I? The way it turned out, I've had to work just as hard and spread my work out over a lot more people who needed me. As for Jonathan and that blond girl, don't you fret. There's much truth in old sayings or they wouldn't be old sayings. There's many a slip 'twixt the cup and the lip—not to mention lots of fish in the sea."

"I reckon so, ma'am."

Major Ella dumped the towel too. She put her hands on her hips. "Well, we've discussed love, haven't we? Now let's talk about duty. Duty comes along in a person's life more than love does, believe me! You may be angry with Jonathan but you and Leo could still go to this saloon for him, couldn't you?" She smiled. "Leo tells me all you Quineys are 'hogs for duty.' "

Beeler pondered, scowling, then said, "Yes, ma'am, I reckon that's so. First of all, I came along to look after my horse; then after that came Quiney duty. Any feeling I used to have for Graber came snailin' in last of all."

"Good! That puts duty first. Even if you don't like Jonathan, you've come many miles with him, and you ought to see this through. My heavens, girl, don't you have any curiosity at all?"

Beeler examined her boots for a spell, teetering on

their high heels, telling herself there was a lot in what the Major said. While the woman took down a sheet, she asked, "Ma'am, do you find it bothersome to be bogged down in carpets?"

"Not when the carpets belong to me! I've been all over the West in one mining town after another, and I expect to be in a lot more. I take up my carpets and go with them." She gave Beeler a severe look over the top of her spectacles. "But I'm the one who decides where my carpets and I go—not my husband or my father or brother."

Beeler brightened. "I guess that's one way to have your carpets and not get bogged down in 'em too."

"Well, that's the way this woman does it. I can't say that not having married made me miss out on being a woman. It seems to me that I do a woman's work as well as a man's. Single blessedness is a lot better than misery in double harness. Everybody isn't cut out for wedlock. Some people are cut up by it. I never had any children of my own, but I've raised fourteen orphans and turned them loose as good people to write me letters now and then."

Beeler exclaimed, "Holy gatlins, that's more kids than my ma and pa had!"

Major Ella nodded as she started struggling with another big white sheet. "And I'm still around to take in more, like the three I have right now. Tell me,

Beulah Land, are you going to this Sundown saloon tomorrow?"

"Yes'm."

"Why? Duty or curiosity?"

Beeler laughed. "Both of 'em, ma'am, though I think our luck'll run muddy."

"Maybe so, child. The pleasure duty brings is generally to the person who does the chore. Having done it is his chief reward. As for satisfying curiosity, that's the real big grab bag in life!"

Mitchell drove the Quineys in the rig to Bartlett the next morning and saw them aboard the train after they'd bought round-trip tickets. Major Ella had fixed them a basket of grub and given Beeler a note to give the proprietor of the Palace Hotel in Gilaville, where they'd stay overnight. She had kept both Leo's Winchester and Beeler's pistol locked up, claiming they wouldn't need them.

The train scared Beeler. The smoking engine was big and black and noisy. The passenger cars were dark red with gold scrollwork on their outsides and scarlet plush on their seats. It made a person nervous just to sit down. And how fast the train went—sometimes as fast as thirty miles an hour, according to the ticket taker.

It took some time to get to Gilaville because the

train wandered north a bit from one little town to
another and sometimes stopped at depots for freight
or to take on water. Beeler watched Arizona Territory
passing from a window on the left side of the train
while Leo watched across the aisle on the right. They
agreed there wasn't much to see—gravelly pinkish
ground, cactus, and sometimes the bright green of
paloverde trees or mesquite.

Midmorning of the next day they reached Gilaville
and got off at the depot, stiff from sitting up all night.
Gilaville was mostly an adobe town too. The most
interesting thing about it was the Colorado River. It
was the biggest, widest bunch of water the Quineys had
ever set eyes on. But looking at it didn't cool a person
off one bit. Gilaville was hell-hinge hot.

A blue-belly soldier from the fort on the bluff over
the river was mighty polite and helpful. He said that
there was a Sundown saloon on the California side and
told them about the ferry over the river.

As she crossed on it with Leo beside her, Beeler ad-
mitted to herself that she was plenty nervous. What
would they say to Mr. Graber if they found him in a
saloon? They hadn't let Nate know they were going on
without him. They'd left the job of telling him to
Major Ella, which was the way she wanted it. Beeler
figured the Major planned to patch things up between
her and Nate. If anybody could do it, she could.

The saloon they were looking for wasn't much to

see. It wasn't even a big one. Facing west under the railroad bridge, it had the words *Cantina Sundown* painted on its adobe front. Two men were sitting in chairs in the shade of its front porch. One was in a straight chair, the other in a rocker. One man was very large and burly, the other one oversize tall and long-shanked with Mexican rowel spurs on his boots. Both men had dark brown beards.

Beeler poked Leo. "That's two of them galoots we been huntin'. We come to the right place." Taking off her hat, she walked up to them, feeling the sun's heat on her back. She was nervous enough to be sweating but wasn't one bit. Sweat dried on a person fast in crackling-dry Arizona Territory in August.

"We're lookin' for a Mr. Graber," she told the biggest man.

"Who'd you be?" he asked sharply.

Beeler took note that he didn't say he didn't *know* any Graber. "Beulah Land Quiney from Santa Rosa County, Texas. This is my brother Leo. We'd like to see Mr. Graber, please."

"Did you come all the way from Texas lookin' for him?" The grasshopper-legged man wanted to know. "How come you'd do such a thing? Are you kin to him?"

"We ain't, but his son is. We come with his son all the way from Texas until yesterday when a steer upped and stepped on his foot in Hard Rock."

"Graber didn't have no living boy," said the big man.

Leo put in, "Yep, he surely does—name of Jonathan, but we call him Nate."

"*Jonathan?*" The tallest man got up out of his rocking chair. He called inside, "Juanito, bring out some lemonade. Put some ice in it."

Ice! That was something to look forward to. Beeler and Leo went up onto the porch to sit on the top step. The tallest man stuck out his hand. "I'm Vincent Owensby, and this is my brother, Ralph. Tell us about this Jonathan."

Beeler noticed how closely the men listened to her while she drank cold lemonade the Mexican boy had brought. She told about Nate's ride down into Mexico after getting a letter from his pa and about him being confused when he found him gone and heard the name Puesta del Sol. And how they'd hunted Sunset and Sundown for weeks and weeks. She didn't ask, but from the way the Owensby brothers acted, they knew Mr. Graber and they were protecting him. He must be wanted. Maybe they all were. She was very careful not to rile them.

Mr. Vincent asked, "What's this here Nate of yours look like, little lady?"

Beeler answered, "Sort of lardy, curly-headed, and pale in the face."

"It has to be Graber's boy," said Mr. Ralph. "And he's alive after all!"

"It's him," said Beeler. Holy gatlins, they seemed to think Nate was dead. Just to identify the older Graber better she asked, "Is this here Graber bald all over his head and used to be curly-headed?"

"He was. Wilberforce Graber was," said Mr. Vincent.

"*Was?* Ain't he bald anymore? Does hair grow back?"

"It don't. Hair never does grow back on a man's head. Wilberforce is who I'm talking about. *He* ain't no more. He's dead. Died three weeks ago. He started to sweat some and then he died."

Beeler shivered to her toes. She put down her lemonade, because after news like that it didn't seem right to go on drinking. Nate was a real "leppie" now. She asked, "Mr. Graber didn't even know his kid was looking for him?"

"No, girlie, he never did," came from Mr. Ralph. "We got news at the mine down near Santa Inez that a yellow-haired gringo boy got shot and killed by bandits. We all figured it was Wilberforce's son on his way to see his old pa. We knew Wilberforce had writ him a letter sayin' where he was and to come down. Some Mexicans buried the yellow-headed boy before Wilberforce got to identify him. There wasn't nothing the boy had that would show anybody who he was."

"It wasn't Nate!" cried Leo.

"Wilberforce and us—we thought sure it was. Wilberforce didn't want no more of Mexico after that. And them bandits was so bad hangin' around after the mine payroll that we lit out the next day after we checked on the boy who got killed. There wasn't any real cause to hang around anymore anyhow. Foremen like us and bookkeepers like Wilberforce draw good pay down there. We had enough money to last each of us awhile, so we left while the going was good. It was safest travelin' together in a band."

Leo interrupted. "Did Mr. Graber leave any cash money for Nate?"

Mr. Vincent looked mournful. "No money at all. He lost all he had in New Mexico Territory. So did Ralph and me."

"Now you be fair to Wilberforce," came from Mr. Ralph. "You and me didn't lose our money the same way he did. We lost ours playin' faro and poker. Wilberforce put his in a hotel safe, and in the night robbers ran off with the safe. That was the end of our money and his. But we got some dandy times outa ours. Wilberforce didn't."

"How come you came here?" asked Beeler. "We had a real hard time findin' Sundown."

"Well, our old pa owns this saloon," came from Mr. Vincent. "Ralph and me, we know what we always do when we get some money in our pokes. Money burns

a hole right through them. We figure we'll lose what
we earn somewheres along the line, and we always do.
Our old pa, he grubstakes us to go out mining again
and make more money. Some places we traveled coming
here from Old Mexico we told folks we met that we
was on our way to Sundown, meaning this here saloon.
But to save Wilberforce from turnin' red in the face
the way he did about saloons, we didn't ever say it was
a Gilaville saloon. We let 'em think it was a real town."

Mr. Vincent paused for a moment and grinned at
them. Then he went on with his story. "We knew
we'd end up here sooner or later, Ralph and me, but
we never reckoned that Wilberforce would, too. It
wasn't what he had in mind before them bandits made
off with the hotel safe and his money. Wilberforce
didn't really have any place else to go, and he didn't
have the heart to start out fresh. He said he'd throw
in his luck with the two of us because none of us was
lucky. He stuck with us, even before we got to New
Mexico Territory, when we got in a bit of a ruckus
along the way. Staying with us after that showed how
Wilberforce had changed since he figured his kid was
dead."

"Ruckus?" Beeler saw how Leo had pricked up his
ears at the word. "Was *Nate's* pa mixed up in a
ruckus?"

"Naw, not Wilberforce. Ruckuses weren't in his

nature. The ruckus was nothin' much. One of us, not Ralph or me, had to shoot and wound a man who tried to steal his horse." Mr. Vincent nodded his head. "The man who got wounded was only winged, but he turned out to be the sheriff's brother, and the sheriff where we was in Texas didn't take it kindly. We got away after we stood off the sheriff and some of his men, but after that we always said we was on our way to Sundown—or most of the time didn't say where we was headed at all. We didn't choose to be trailed."

Beeler said, "It's too bad you only winged the sheriff's no-good brother. I get worked up easy when it comes to horse thieves. Where would them other galoots be?"

Mr. Ralph scratched his ear. "They hung onto their money. Slept on top of it wherever we went and never went near no faro tables. They went on to the Pacific coast. They been gone quite a while now. Someday when I find somebody willin' to do it I'll have a letter writ them tellin' 'em Wilberforce passed over the Great Divide and into the Great Unknown."

"How come he didn't go with them?" asked Beeler.

"He didn't seem to have the heart to budge from here. And he didn't have the stomach for it neither. Nothin' he ate agreed with him all the time we was on the trail. The trip here tuckered him out somethin' terrible. It's lotsa miles from Santa Inez down in Mexico to here."

"Where's he buried?" Leo wanted to know.

"In the nice graveyard over the river. We gave him a good funeral—a dandy send-off with the Gilaville String Band playin' tunes he used to favor."

"He was a Texan," said Beeler. "Once a Texan, always a Texan. He shoulda been laid to rest in Texas dirt."

"Now that woulda been hard to arrange, girlie," said Mr. Ralph.

"Mebbe so. It's a long way from here to Santa Rosa County." Beeler rested her elbows on her knees and put her chin into her hands. "Us Quineys woulda been honored to have Mr. Graber, a wisdom bringer, down by the creek in our family graveyard. It's my plan someday to have Nate restin' in it. Mebbe."

The Owensby brothers, Westerners too, looked at each other nodding their heads. They understood.

Suddenly Leo asked again, "Didn't old man Graber leave anythin' to Nate—not even his horse and saddle and hogleg?"

"There wasn't hardly anythin' to leave. You gotta remember, too, we thought his kid was dead. We sold the horse and saddle to buy Wilberforce a headstone. His pistol never did have a hammer on it. He just wore it for show."

"He's got a headstone?" Beeler wanted to know.

"Sure he has. A nice one, with *W. W. Graber 1834-1881* carved on it."

"Has it got an angel on top?" Leo asked.

"Nope, no angel. That cost too much money. It's white marble, though."

Beeler nodded. Nate would like that. She doubted if he would come to Gilaville to see the headstone for himself, though. She didn't think he'd have the heart for it.

For a while there was a mournful silence. Then Mr. Vincent answered Leo's question, sounding very sad. "All we got left of dear old Wilberforce is a Bible and a watch. They're still around here someplace. He was flat broke as a salted snail when we got here. Do you suppose his kid would want the book and the time-piece? The watch ain't even gold."

Beeler spoke up. "Yes, sir, we'd like to take him somethin' that was his pa's."

"You wait. I'll fetch 'em for ya. We didn't know what to do with 'em so we just kept 'em. We'd be honored if you'd take 'em." Mr. Ralph heaved himself up. He was back in a little while with a plain black-bound Bible and an ordinary-looking silver case watch.

Mr. Ralph stared at the two Quineys on the front steps for a long solemn moment, looking from face to face. He handed the Bible to Leo, then the watch to Beeler.

Beeler studied the tracings of ivy leaves on the face of the watchcase, then turned it over to see *WWG* on its back. She pressed the little spring along its side, and it flipped open, the way men's pocket watches did. Music came out—the pretty tune of "Evalina." With Leo watching over her shoulder, Beeler examined what else there was in the watchcase besides the timepiece itself. On one side of it there was a picture of a lady with a lock of light brown hair curled around it. She had a sweet smile and her hair was pulled back in a way that was out of style now when most ladies wore frizzled bangs. The picture looked to be old. Nate's ma, for sure! The lady had a smile a lot like his, come to think on it.

"Thank you kindly," said Beeler, putting the watch into her shirt pocket where it would be safe. She got up. "I guess Leo and me are satisfied now that we found the right Sundown," she told the Owensbys.

The brothers got up, too. Mr. Vincent said, "We wish to God we had better news for ya to take back to Graber's boy."

Beeler told him, "It ain't your fault his pa died."

"It surely ain't. We got a doctor from Gilaville for him when he took sick."

"Mebbe it was the doctor's fault he died!" Leo said. "Some doctors know horses better'n they know folks."

"This wasn't that kind of doc. One thing doctors can't mend is busted hearts. Wilberforce took it mighty hard when he heard he'd lost his kid. He was always a silent cuss. But after that he got silenter and politer. Them are bad signs in most folks. I surely hope his boy don't take the news that hard."

"Well, mebbe he'll try to," came from Beeler, "but Leo and me will talk him out of it, and if we can't, Major Gordon ought to be able to. She talks good cow sense."

Mr. Vincent started to laugh. "We know her. Who don't in these parts? There ain't nothin' like her. She can argue a second man to death while the first one's in the hospital slowly recoverin'."

Beeler poked Leo to get him up off the porch. She said, "*Adiós,* Mister and Mister. We'll leave now."

"*Gracias* for the lemon squeezin's," said Leo.

After they'd walked away a couple of steps, the girl turned around to call back, "Hey, was Mr. Graber a old whiskey soak?"

"He never touched a drop," said Mr. Ralph.

Beeler pondered some. They'd already said he didn't carry a pistol that worked, and he didn't gamble. She called out again, "Did he do anythin' that was bad?"

"Not that we ever saw!" came from Mr. Vincent. "You might say he was a saint. Mighty hard to live with!"

"Mighty hard!" agreed Mr. Ralph.

Beeler nodded. She'd be sure to tell Nate all those things about his pa. They'd pleasure him, but she doubted if they'd make him any easier to live with either. She'd have to think a bit before she tied up with a saint.

Speaking of saints made a body think about angels. Before they climbed back on that train, she and Leo would pay a visit to the Gilaville graveyard. They'd check Mr. Graber's headstone, not that she didn't believe the Owensby brothers had got one for him. White marble sounded mighty fine. Maybe she and Leo would make up a story to tickle Nate that there was an angel standing on top of the headstone, an angel with wings and a trumpet. But somehow she doubted if Leo would go along with the lie. He probably would say it wasn't the right thing to do to Nate. Besides, Nate might get the idea to come here on the train, too, to see an angel that wasn't there.

The two Quineys went side by side to the banks of the Colorado where they stood waiting for the ferry to come back to the California side. For a fact, they hadn't been long in California. But it was a new place they'd visited, and it would make a good story back home.

While they waited, Beeler opened Mr. Graber's watch to hear "Evalina" another time. She remembered that tune. That was the very one she and Nate had danced to in the mountain meadow the night the Apaches had come. She might never corner Nate and

reform him to Quiney ways. She might marry somebody else. Or she might never take on double-harness
hitching at all!

Whatever she did, though, she'd learned one thing
from all the traveling around she'd done. She wouldn't
be hasty about getting hitched. She was going to see
some of the world first. She recalled what poor lonesome Mr. McCarty had said about wanting to see
England. Well, she might just go there someday. She'd
learned a thing or two wandering around with Nate
Graber. And whenever she heard "Evalina," she knew
he'd come to mind. That was something nice to think
of a person by—a tune!

Beeler and Leo got onto the ferry and stood on the
deck, again spitting together down into the brown
water of the Colorado. Beeler looked at Leo out of the
corner of one eye. He wasn't so bad a brother after all.
He'd saved her from having to ask the Owensby
brothers to cough up what Nate's pa had left to him.
Leo had taken it on himself to be bad mannered,
which had been right noble of him. And he hadn't said
one word to her after they'd left the saloon steps about
how she'd been the one to make up the big story that
the five men were bandit desperadoes. She supposed
he'd tell Nate, though, that she'd been wrong. Well,
she'd just have to grin and bear what Nate would say
to her.

She gazed at the Colorado, rushing south toward Old Mexico. It was sure in a hurry for a river. Well, that didn't mean she had to be in a rush to settle her life. But she guessed now might be a good time to settle something with Leo.

She said, "Leo, I think in time I could forgive ya for lockin' me up in that root cellar and for stealin' Jingle-bob. In a way you mebbe done me a favor. If you hadn't run off with him, I'd never have got to see so much of the world. I'd still be down in Santa Rosa County with the weaner gals and Nerissa tryin' to keep Travis from bustin' down the front porch. Even if you're a two-time horse stealer, I think I'll be able to forgive ya."

AUTHOR'S NOTE

After librarians and teachers had asked me for a number of years to write a book for boys, I complied with *A Long Way to Whiskey Creek*. But though I took Parker Quiney and Jonathan Graber all over Texas in 1879, I didn't forget the "womenfolks stuck to home." Those nineteenth-century Texas women were every bit as strong as their men.

I like to think of this book as a companion piece to the earlier one about the Quineys. Beulah Land Quiney does not appear in that one. Leo is mentioned only briefly in its first chapter along with Nerissa. Jonathan Graber and J.E.B. Stuart are the only characters common to both novels.

Readers tell me they like to know what is fact and what is fiction in historical novels. Many things in this story are fact.

To begin with, Texas readers might rise up in wrath

at the thought that I overlooked the existence of a
Sundown in northwest Texas, the very territory my
characters search in. Sundown, Texas, did not exist—
at least by that name—in 1881. It was laid out in 1928
and had its first store in 1929. For this information I
an indebted to Sara E. Niles of the Reference Staff
of the Lubbock Public Library.

The towns mentioned in the novel have fictional
names, although they are based on real places and real
descriptions. My young Texans crossed real rivers.

It would not have been at all impossible for Beeler,
Leo, and Nate to have met Billy the Kid under one of
his aliases, Henry McCarty. He was in this particular
part of New Mexico Territory in late June/early July,
1881. He is described as eyewitnesses knew him—lithe
and small, ambidextrous, and supposedly able to do
remarkable things with a pistol. Wanted as a horse
thief and a murderer, he had escaped from jail in
Lincoln, New Mexico Territory, that same spring.
It is a fact that he liked an Englishman, John H. Tunstall, who had been his employer in 1878. Tunstall's
murder drove Billy to outlawry. Although pursued by
John Poe, Billy the Kid was shot to death on July 14,
1881, by a man named Pat Garrett. Until Garrett
published a book about Billy in 1882, the Kid was
known chiefly in New Mexico Territory. His is an ex-
ample of a literary reputation.

Circuses were not at all unknown in the Old West, odd as it may seem. A woman named Annie Sylvester was a noted bicyclienne in the 1880's. Marvelous Melinda is based on her. Miss Sylvester was the first woman to ride a unicycle and for this feat received a diamond-studded gold medal from the San Francisco and Oakland Bicycle Club as the World's Champion Trick and Fancy Bicyclienne. Annie Sylvester trouped with fifteen different circuses. She did indeed drive a chariot and participated in chariot races. She worked with lions, as many as six at a time. Miss Sylvester, who reputedly guarded herself from bandits by carrying a Colt .45 in her muff, lived in Southern California during her later years and died in 1938. An account of her life can be found in *True West* magazine, August, 1972.

Camels would have been familiar animals to people in the Southwest in the 1880's. The Federal government imported them in the 1850's, thinking that they would adapt to the Sonora and Mojave deserts. During the Civil War a camel driver from Syria carried military dispatches on camelback from Fort Yuma, Arizona Territory, to the pueblo of Los Angeles, California. The camel experiment was no great success—chiefly because horses and mules cannot abide the company of camels. Some were released to forage for themselves in the desert. Others were sold to circuses or down into Old Mexico. Wild camels roamed the West for many years.

New Mexico Territory was a haven for wanted men from Texas. This added to the general dislike of Texans, as well as the fact that the New Mexicans felt for many years that Texas was about to annex their territory.

The saloon sign Nate commits to memory existed, though I have no idea what sort of burial insurance plan the management had.

Skunks were far more feared in the Old West than people would ever believe. They were sometimes rabid and, seeking warmth, would get into a man's bed with him during cattle drives, when cowboys slept on the ground. The Pasteur treatment for rabies was not developed until 1885. Before that, contracting hydrophobia was indeed a death sentence. Skunks have many characteristics of the cat, and one particular pet skunk delighted in eating the "holes" in doughnuts, punched out of the raw dough before the doughnuts are deep-fried. (Doughnuts were much indulged in in old Texas. The hole was needed to make them truly "finger food." They were a cowboy's delight.)

"High-grading" was a name for stealing very rich ore from a mine. There is a true story of a man who claimed to be bringing a letter and instead stayed to rob his host.

Major Ella Gordon is fictional in this story. The woman on whom she is based was real—Miss Nellie Cashman, commonly referred to as Colonel Nellie. She was one of the most remarkable women of the Old West. Born in Ireland, she ran boardinghouses all over the West—in Canada, Idaho Territory, Nevada, Arizona Territory, and Alaska. Colonel Nellie never married. In her own words, she considered men to be "nuisances." Renowned for her good deeds, the rearing of orphans, founding of hospitals, and welfare work with the destitute and prisoners, she died in 1925. *The West* magazine of July, 1972, carries a very interesting article about her.

Travis's behavior is pretty much that of a typical hand-raised longhorn. Readers might be entertained and educated by *The Longhorns* by J. Frank Dobie. There is also an interesting article, "Those Amazing Texas Longhorns," by Charles J. Haluska, in a 1970 issue of *Southland,* a pictorial supplement to the Long Beach (Calif.) *Independent.* It features the herd of 106 longhorns living today in California. A rancher, whose real business is raising grapevines, maintains the herd as a hobby and considers the cattle "interesting characters." They hate dogs and umbrellas and seem to favor music.

The medical remedies mentioned in this novel were actually employed. Sulphur, molasses, and cream of tartar as a blood purifier was a very common remedy. Sassafras tea thinned blood, while rusty nail water supplied iron for it. Morley's Vitalizer could be bought in general stores. Goose grease gizzard oil was for chest colds, turpentine and lard for coughs.

The Quineys could have traveled on the Southern Pacific Railroad across Arizona Territory in 1881. They could have crossed the Colorado River by rail-road bridge at Yuma and gone into California. They would have found the Colorado River a far broader and more unruly stream than it now is. Today it is dammed.

In researching *How Many Miles to Sundown*, I've used a number of books. I will list only those that deal with the humor, wit, and language of the period. Ramon Adams is the author of several of them: *The Oldtime Cowhand*, *The Best of the American Cowboy*, *The Cowboy and His Humor*, and *Burs Under the Saddle*. I also drew on *The Log of a Cowboy* by Andy Adams, *The Cowboy Reader* edited by Lon Tinkle and A. Maxwell, and *From the Pecos to the Powder* by Bob Kennon and Ramon Adams.

As usual, the Beatty-bedeviled reference staffs of the Riverside Public Library and University of Cali-fornia (Riverside) Library were queried on various topics. I thank a number of librarians for their search-ings—whether fruitful or no. I must also say thank you to Ella Jahnke and Howard Hays, Jr. (a real-life news-paper editor) for saying they would like to "be" in my book.

Dr. Myra Ellen Jenkins, archivist of the State of New Mexico, also deserves my gratitude for research. Lastly, I should acknowledge my debt to my husband, Dr. John Beatty, and teen-age daughter, Alexandra, for listening to *How Many Miles to Sundown* being read aloud, chapter by chapter, as the book progressed. They criticized every other word! Someday I shall thank them.

Patricia Beatty
January 1973

ABOUT THE AUTHOR

Now a resident of Southern California, Patricia Beatty was born in Portland, Oregon. She was graduated from Reed College, and then taught high-school English and history for four years. Later she held various positions as science and technical librarian. Recently she taught Writing Fiction for Children in the Extension Department of the University of California, Los Angeles. She has had a number of historical novels published by Morrow, several of them dealing with the American West in the 1860 to 1895 period.

Mrs. Beatty has lived in Coeur d'Alene, Idaho; London, England; and Wilmington, Delaware, as well as on the West Coast. Her husband, Dr. John Beatty, her co-author for a number of books, teaches the history of England at a major California university. One of their books, *The Royal Dirk*, was chosen as an Award book by the Southern California Council on Children's and Young People's Literature. The Beattys have a teen-age daughter, Alexandra.